"*Bob? Did you hear me?*"

He shook his head to clear his thoughts and gave her a shy grin. "Yeah, I heard you."

Moving back around the desk, she gracefully seated herself before smoothing at her hair. "You and I have always been a good team, haven't we?"

"I've always thought so."

She lowered her head a bit and batted her long, dark lashes. "When I was a little girl, I used to drape a scarf over my head and pretend the two of us were getting married. Isn't that funny?"

Her words startled him. "Would that have been so bad?"

"Marrying you? No, of course not. But you never loved me. You married Lydia."

"You went to New York. Life went on. I met Lydia and fell in love with her. The rest is history."

"If—if you hadn't met Lydia—"

"You wouldn't have married me, El. We both know that. You wanted to make your mark in the world. You set a goal for yourself, and you went after it."

"I might have married you, if you'd waited for me."

"I could never have offered you what old Mr. Scrooge did. You're an elegant woman, El, with elegant tastes. I'll never be more than an accountant." He gave her a weak ———— d a part-time Webmaster, thanks to ———————— lia and I had a good life. I lo———————— he children we had together———————— her desk. "You might look————————

El was silent for a mo———————— loved me as much as you l————————

"I've always loved you, E—— ——————— always will."

"But not in the same way you loved her?"

He moved slowly toward the door. "Hard to say. You never gave me a chance."

JOYCE LIVINGSTON has done many things in her life (in addition to being a wife, mother of six, and grandmother to oodles of grandkids, all of whom she loves dearly). From being a television broadcaster for eighteen years, to lecturing and teaching on quilting and sewing, to writing magazine articles on a variety of subjects. She's danced with Lawrence Welk, ice-skated with a chimpanzee, had bottles broken over her head by stuntmen, interviewed hundreds of celebrities and controversial figures, and many other interesting and unusual things. But now, when she isn't off traveling to wonderful and exotic places as a part-time tour escort, her days are spent sitting in front of her computer, creating stories. She feels her writing is a ministry and a calling from God, and she hopes Heartsong readers will be touched and uplifted by what she writes. Joyce loves to hear from her readers and invites you to visit her on the Internet at: www.joycelivingston.com

Books by Joyce Livingston

Don't miss out on any of our super romances. Write to us at the following address for information on our newest releases and club information.

Heartsong Presents Readers' Service
PO Box 721
Uhrichsville, OH 44683

Or visit www.heartsongpresents.com

Bah Humbug, Mrs. Scrooge

Joyce Livingston

Heartsong Presents

This book is dedicated to Heartline Literary Agent Joyce Hart and her husband Jim, two marvelous people God sent into my life when my husband became ill and I really needed them. I will be eternally grateful for the way God miraculously brought the four of us together on a cruise ship to Hawaii. He is truly a God of miracles. As with every book I write now, it is also dedicated to my hero, my wonderful husband who recently went to heaven to be with our Lord. I miss you, Don, and always will.

And I can't forget all of you thoughtful, concerned readers who have supported me with your sweet letters and emails as you've learned about Don's homegoing. Your outpouring of love and encouragement have touched my heart. Thank you for caring.

A note from the Author:
I love to hear from my readers! You may correspond with me by writing:

Joyce Livingston
Author Relations
PO Box 719
Uhrichsville, OH 44683

ISBN 1-59310-655-6

BAH HUMBUG, MRS. SCROOGE

Copyright © 2005 by Joyce Livingston. All rights reserved. Except for use in any review, the reproduction or utilization of this work in whole or in part in any form by any electronic, mechanical, or other means, now known or hereafter invented, is forbidden without the permission of Heartsong Presents, an imprint of Barbour Publishing, Inc., PO Box 719, Uhrichsville, Ohio 44683.

All scripture quotations are taken from the King James Version of the Bible.

All of the characters and events in this book are fictitious. Any resemblance to actual persons, living or dead, or to actual events is purely coincidental.

Our mission is to publish and distribute inspirational products offering exceptional value and biblical encouragement to the masses.

PRINTED IN THE U.S.A.

prologue

"Come on, you big scaredy-cat." Eight-year-old Eleanor Baker stuck out her tongue at her closest friend and neighbor as she stepped out onto the ice, testing it with a little jump. "Don't be such a big baby. It'll be fun!"

Shaking his head, Bobby Rachette plunked himself down on a nearby log, disgust clouding his face. "I don't think we should, El, that ice looks pretty thin. What if we fall through?"

Eleanor gave her head a flip then buttoned the top button on her parka. "Go ahead. Walk all the way around the pond if you're afraid. I don't need you, Bobby. I can go by myself!"

"You'd better not." Leaving his book bag on the ground, he struggled to his feet. "My mom said I should never go out on the ice unless my dad checks it first."

Planting her gloved hands on her hips, she jutted out her chin defiantly. "Well, it looks okay to me. See? I'm not falling through."

He grabbed her hand and pulled her back then, shoving her behind him, spread his arms open wide, blocking her way. "Let me test it first. I weigh more than you do."

Eleanor wrapped her arms across her chest and shivered. "Okay, but you better hurry. I'm getting cold."

Carefully, he put one foot out on the ice then the other, and tested it with a small jump. "I guess it's not cracking."

She responded with a flip of her head and a smirk. "See, I told you it was thick enough. Just because you're better at arithmetic than I am doesn't mean you're smarter than me."

A skeptical frown screwed up his face. "I don't know, El."

Using more force, he pounded his feet down hard. "It seems okay, but my dad says the ice might not be as thick out where the water is deeper. I think we'd better walk around the pond like we always do. What if it'd crack and we'd—"

Eleanor gave her head an arrogant toss. "It looks fine to me. Go ahead! Walk all the way around if you want to. I'm crossing here." Planting her palms on his chest and giving him a shove, she moved quickly past him and ran farther out onto the ice, calling back over her shoulder, "I'll beat you to the other side, slowpoke!"

"Come back, El! You're being really dumb," Bobby yelled after her, but Eleanor ignored his warning.

She moved quickly across the glassy surface, taking long strides like an ice skater as a chilling breeze wrapped its icy tentacles around her and made her quiver. "You're such a baby!" she called out with a frosty giggle.

"El! Did you hear me? Come back!"

"No! I'm having too much fun." Grinning, she stopped momentarily and turned toward Bobby's voice. He was standing at the edge of the pond, book bag in hand, looking glum and waving at her. "Go on! Walk all the way around. See if I care!" she shouted in a taunting voice, giving him a mocking flip of her hand. "Nanny, nanny, boo-boo! Bobby is a scaredy-cat!"

"Your dad's gonna whop you when he finds you went out on the ice!"

"Then you better not tell him!"

"Please, El! Come back. You're scaring me."

But Eleanor didn't want to go back. When she made up her mind to do something, no one, not even her father—who beat her unmercifully when she disobeyed—could stop her. She had the scars to prove it, too. Bobby had seen the welts and bruises on her arms and legs. So had his mother, many times, and she'd threatened to call the authorities. But Eleanor had begged her not to, reminding her that if she did, her father said he would not only take his anger out on her, but her mother and older sister, Eileen, as well. She'd rather take the beatings than have him hurt either one of them. He was an awful man and nothing like Bobby's father.

Fortunately, her father, who was rarely at home, preferred to spend most of his unemployed days at the local bar, giving his family a few hours of much-needed peace. But when he came roaring into the house, drunk and going into a fit of rage over the least little thing, they all ran for cover. She had counted the days until she would be old enough to run away from home and escape the cruel beatings and his abusive mouth. No man was ever going to treat her like that! She'd never be dependent on someone else to take care of her. She was going to make it on her own.

The air whipped across the pond with bone-chilling force as Eleanor slid across the ice, pretending to be the star of an ice show. She imagined herself wearing a sparkly blue dress and beautiful white skates—the kind she'd seen in the Christmas catalog at Bobby's house—as she whirled and twirled gracefully across the arena with thousands of people wildly clapping, some even throwing flowers out onto the ice like she'd seen them do on TV. What fun she was having. If only Bobby had come with her—they could hold hands and spin around together.

Suddenly, she stopped, ceasing all motion. What was that sound?

❧

Bobby watched until El was halfway across the frozen pond then, after pulling his stocking cap down over his ears, buttoned the top button on his jacket. Adjusting his hold on his book bag, he started around the edge of the pond, sending an occasional glance in Eleanor's direction. Maybe he should have gone with her. She'd be on the other side long before he was. Besides, look at all the fun she was having gliding across the ice. Eleanor was the brave one, the one who was always willing to do risky things, like climb that skinny tree out in their backyard. Despite his warning, she'd climbed clear to the top, way up high where the branches were thin and yielding, and had fallen, breaking her arm when she'd hit the ground. Then there was the time she'd scaled old Mr. Harvey's fence to get their baseball and been bitten by his dog. . . .

"Bobby! Help!"

His friend's hair-raising scream sent him scurrying toward the pond.

"The ice is cracking!"

His mind raced. "Don't move, El!"

"I'm afraid! It's making a funny noise!" she screamed shakily. "Help me, Bobby!"

The fear in her voice terrified him. What should he do? Go for help? What if the ice broke and she fell through while he was gone?

Feeling totally helpless, he glanced around quickly, hoping to find someone nearby, but no one was in sight. *Help me, God! Don't let El fall through the ice!*

"Bobby, help me! I'm scared!"

What? What can I do? He surveyed the area, looking for anything that might help save her life. "I'll help you, El! Don't move!" he shouted, horrified at what might happen but wanting to encourage her. Wasn't he always the one who came to her rescue when she was in trouble? He couldn't let her down now! Not when her life may depend on him.

Show me, God! Show me how to help her. Don't let her die!

There it was! The answer he needed. A partially buried, long, rotting length of a weathered board, its tip barely peeking out from under a span of dense growth at the edge of the pond.

Bobby tugged with all his might and finally the board broke loose, letting him fall backward. "I'm coming, El!"

Afraid the ice would not hold his weight and El's, especially with the addition of the board, Bobby moved quickly to the pond, dropped nervously to his stomach, and inched his way toward the frightened Eleanor, pushing the board ahead of him.

"Please hurry, Bobby! I think the ice is cracking more!"

The terrified look on her face was all it took to make him move a little faster. "I'm almost there. Get down on your stomach then grab the end of the board when I push it toward you. Don't push on the ice; just let me drag you."

Trembling, she did as she was told.

Bobby began to scoot backward toward the shore, pulling the board and Eleanor along with him.

When they were finally safe and on solid ground, Eleanor threw her arms around Bobby's neck and began to cry.

"It's okay," he told her, wiping his nose on his sleeve. "I'd never let anything happen to you, El. You're my best friend."

one

Twenty-five years later

"I'm sorry, Mrs. Scrooge. I'll never let it happen again. I—I never thought about showing her the matching sweater."

Pointing an elegantly manicured finger toward the costly cashmere sweater, Eleanor glared at the woman. "Do you realize you've just cost Scrooge's Fashions a big sale? That customer would have bought that sweater, but, thanks to your ineptness, she didn't even know it existed." She paused, giving her words time to soak in. "You're new, so I'm going to overlook it this time, but see to it you never let it happen again. Ask any of my employees; I'm not famous for giving second chances."

"I promise I won't let it happen again." The embarrassed woman lowered her head, avoiding her boss's eyes. "Thank you, Mrs. Scrooge."

"She's only worked for Scrooge's a few weeks," Karen Small, the fashion department manager said, apologizing as the chastised clerk backed away. "I'm sure it never occurred to her to show the customer the matching sweater."

Eleanor stopped and stared at Karen, her brow creased. "Then you need to accept half of the blame. It's your job to make sure our employees are properly trained."

Karen started to protest but wisely let the words die on her lips. Eleanor didn't tolerate back talk from her staff.

"See to it you work with her." Eleanor bent and picked up a gum wrapper from the floor. "Need I remind you that our business is glamour and style? Our customers depend on Scrooge's to provide them with the latest fashions. I've structured this store to be a one-stop shopping experience for the most fastidious women and help others raise their fashion standards. We're here to outfit them from head to toe—from beautiful jewelry to cosmetics to shoes and everything in between. They expect us to give them guidance. That customer needed that matching sweater. We did her a disservice by not showing it to her and giving her an opportunity to purchase it."

"I'm aware of that, Mrs. Scrooge. But it takes time to train a—"

"Please. No excuses." Eleanor rolled her eyes and held her flattened palm toward Karen, allowing her words to take on an even icier tone for effect. "Remember, Karen, the salespeople in your department are a reflection of you. If they don't look good, you don't look good. I promoted you to manager of your department because I thought you were capable of handling the position. See to it you don't disappoint me again."

"Excuse me!" A matronly woman waved her hand at the pair as she came out of a fitting room wearing a gorgeous, chartreuse tunic embellished with big, red, sequin-trimmed roses. "Do you think white pants would look better than the chartreuse pair? I'm afraid maybe this is too much color for me."

Karen moved to the woman's side immediately. "The chartreuse pants look wonderful on you, ma'am. The continuation of the chartreuse from your shoulders to your ankles creates an almost monochromatic look, giving you a long, fluid, complementary line." She gave a glance back over her shoulder at Eleanor, as if to say, "See? I do know my business."

The woman moved to one of the nearby mirrors and began to turn from one way to the other, admiring the fit and color of the garments. "I see what you mean. I'll take both pieces."

"You really look lovely in that color." Eleanor moved up close and stood gazing admiringly into the mirror over the woman's shoulder. "It's very smart of you to take both the chartreuse and the white pants. Think of the versatility they will give you. It will be like having two entirely different outfits, and white always looks so crisp and cool. Will you be wearing these on a cruise?"

The customer smiled and nodded at Eleanor's reflection. "Yes, in two weeks. My husband and I are celebrating our fortieth anniversary."

Eleanor raised her eyes, feigning surprise. "Your fortieth anniversary? Really? My, you don't look a day older than fifty! Surely you didn't get married when you were ten!"

"I'm sixty-five," the woman said proudly.

"I never would have guessed it. You look so young. A fortieth wedding anniversary is a very special occasion. What are you going to wear to the captain's formal night reception?"

Turning from the mirror, the woman gave her a puzzled stare. "I haven't decided. I have a nice black cocktail dress. I thought I'd wear either a string of pearls with it or maybe a sequined chiffon scarf of some sort."

Eleanor reached for her hand. "Come with me. I have something you must see." Adrenaline pumped through her body. She loved an opportunity to show off her salesmanship—the thing that had made Everett Scrooge sit up and take notice of her many years ago when she'd first been hired on at Scrooge's. She led the woman to the evening wear section and seated her in one of the plush velvet slipper chairs. "You sit right there and let me show you what I think would be perfect for that cruise of yours." She gave the woman her best winsome smile. "It's not every day you get to celebrate your fortieth anniversary."

Two hours later, Eleanor stood beside her customer as the woman prepared to exit the store after having purchased seven outfits, seven pairs of shoes, three handbags, a variety of lingerie, a new bathing suit with matching pareo, two nightgowns with matching robes, bedroom slippers, three pairs of chandelier earrings with matching necklaces, a bottle of very expensive perfume, and an anniversary gift for her husband. "Your husband is going to be so proud of you! I know you'll have a wonderful time on your cruise. Your lovely new things will be delivered to your home on Thursday."

The woman gave her an appreciative smile. "I can't thank you enough for all your help, Mrs. Scrooge. You're a fashion genius."

Eleanor found herself beaming. "Thank you, Mrs. Cahill. I do try to stay informed. My trips to Paris keep me abreast of fashion trends long before they come to the United States." She conjured up her best smile. "It was my pleasure to assist you. I'm here anytime you need me. Now don't forget the appointment we set up in our new beauty salon for next week to have your hair cut and colored."

"I won't!" The woman waved as she stepped outside.

Eleanor watched until Mrs. Cahill disappeared from sight then hurried back to find Karen. "I hope you were watching," she told her when she found her redressing a mannequin. "What could have been a minor sale turned into one of the biggest of the day by using a little salesmanship."

"But all she was shopping for was a tunic and pants!" Karen countered, shrugging her slim shoulders. "She never mentioned needing any of those other items. That was remarkable salesmanship, Mrs. Scrooge."

"That tunic set may have been all she came in for, but not all she needed. What she really needed were eye-catching clothes to take on the cruise to celebrate her anniversary and make her husband proud of her." Eleanor glanced at her watch. "I'm exactly two hours and nineteen minutes behind schedule, thanks to you and your inept associate. If you two had done your jobs, I wouldn't have had to do it for you. It might be a good idea for you to purchase some books on salesmanship. What you learn you can pass on to the ladies in your department. I want this to be the best year Scrooge's has ever had, and we're depending on your department to be the major part of it."

Without waiting for a response, Eleanor made her way to her office at the far end of the second floor of the three-building complex known as Scrooge's. "Send Bob into my office and hold my calls," she barked out at Ruthie, her assistant of ten years, as she passed by her desk. "And get that awful-looking plant off your desk. It looks like a leftover from a funeral."

Being one of the few who didn't quake when Eleanor spoke, Ruthie snickered. "Well, aren't we in a good mood today."

"I should be. I just turned a minor sale into a bonanza," she called back, smiling victoriously over her shoulder. After closing her door, she hurried into the little powder room she'd added when she'd bought their latest building and applied a new coat of lipstick and a dab of powder, something she did with regularity. As the president and CEO of one of the finest and most exclusive women's fashion and department stores in the northeast, she was determined to look the part at all times.

"You wanted to see me?" a male voice asked as the door to her office opened a crack.

She placed her makeup in the drawer, turned off the light, and walked toward her desk with a practiced stance that would put any model to shame, motioning to a chair on her way. "Are we going to make our projection this week?" she asked, sitting down in the tapestry-covered desk chair.

He pulled a paper from a file folder and handed it to her. "I've already run the totals. If the weekend holds up, I'd say we'll finish about eight percent over our projection."

She perused the paper carefully. "Umm, not bad, but we could do better."

"You've already set each department's quota so high the sales staff is in a panic. Maybe you should ease up a bit, El."

Her jaw dropped. "Ease up? Why? We'll never make our projections that way."

"You can't ride people like you do without some adverse reactions. I've heard rumblings that several of your key salespeople are already thinking about leaving. They feel your expectations are way too high for a community this size. Some have even talked about leaving Newport. They say there are plenty of other high-end department stores in this part of the country that would love to hire people with their experience."

Eleanor huffed. "Only because they've worked for me! I have a highly respected reputation in the fashion business, Bob, and I intend to keep it. If people can't produce, I don't need them. One can't stand still and succeed. A successful business has to keep growing, expanding, and trying new things. Scrooge's is known for its innovative way of operating."

"And for its pressure on its department heads and sales-people." He leaned back in the chair and frowned at her over steepled fingers. "Mark my words, El, you're going to lose some great people if you don't cut them a little slack."

Giving him a coy smile, she thumped her pencil on her desk. "If I didn't owe you, Bobby Rachette, I'd fire you for insubordination."

"You don't owe me, El." A shy grin played at his lips. "How many times do I have to tell you? I only did what any kid would have done when his best friend was in trouble."

Eleanor leaned her head against the tall back of her chair and, rotating her fingers against her temples, closed her eyes. "I'll never be able to repay you, Bob. Even after all those things I said about you being a scaredy-cat, you still came after me. You put your own life on the line for me that day at the pond. I could have died if you hadn't come after me. We both could have died."

"But we didn't, El. God protected us. He's the One who

showed me that old board someone left on the beach. I'm just thankful the ice didn't break when I reached it to you."

"Don't give God all the credit. You were the one who was smart enough to lie on your stomach to distribute your weight as you pushed it out toward me. That was a stroke of genius for an eight-year-old."

"Nothing genius about it. God gave me the idea, and He kept the ice from cracking any more until I could get out to where you were."

"I was so afraid. Just thinking about it, even now, makes me tremble. It seemed with each breath I took I could hear it cracking a little more." Blinking hard, she lowered her hands and stared at him. "I still have nightmares about that day."

"You were my friend."

"And you were mine. The best friend I've ever had. You still are." She gestured toward the paper on her desk, the one he'd given her. "You're the only one I can trust."

He harrumphed. "Because I'm the only one who truly knows the real you—the scared little girl who, from the absolute bottom of the barrel with sheer desire and determination, made it to the top."

She released a heavy sigh. "Thanks to Everett Scrooge. You and I both know if he hadn't taken me under his wing after you got me that job in the shipping room, I would never have had the opportunities I've had."

"You made your own opportunities, El. I've never seen anyone work as hard as you have. That's what caught Everett Scrooge's attention. He took one look at your beautiful face and knew you belonged in the cosmetic department instead of the shipping room."

"Still, if it hadn't been for Everett—"

He nodded. "Granted, the old man helped you, but you've always had more drive and stamina than most folks, El. People like you make it, in spite of the odds. Even if you hadn't won that old man's love and he hadn't asked you to marry him, you would have still made it to the top. I'm sure of it."

She fingered the four-carat diamond ring on her left hand. "I did love that old man, Bob. Most people think I married him for his money so I'd inherit everything. While I admit most of that is true, I married him because I respected him and enjoyed being with him. He had a marvelous mind and an unrivaled business savvy. He ran Scrooge's like a well-oiled machine. I was fortunate he took a liking to me. Working side by side with him every day was much better than the college education I couldn't have afforded."

Bob leaned forward, bracing his elbows on his knees, a slight smile curling up the corners of his mouth. "A liking? That's an understatement. That old man was crazy about you. Everyone knew it. And, yes, not only his three nephews resented his fascination with you, but many of the employees resented you, too. It still troubles me that some believed you had a part in his death by not making him take the treatments the doctors had told him were necessary if he wanted to live."

The reminder rankled her. "Everett Scrooge was a strong-willed man. Everyone knew that. The decision to do without the chemotherapy and radiation was his and his alone. I only went along with it because he wanted me to. If those nephews of his had loved their uncle and had come around more when he was sick instead of waiting until he was on his deathbed like a bunch of greedy vultures, they may have gotten some of his money. But they didn't. I was the one who was there for him. None of them were available when he needed them. They didn't deserve one penny. The idea that they thought I should go against their uncle's wishes and give them a portion of Everett's holdings infuriated me!"

Bob seemed to consider her words carefully. "I'm sure, in their hearts, they knew they didn't do right by their uncle. They might not have understood why he left the bulk of his estate to you when the two of you had been married such a short time, but they had to respect your drive, ambition, and desire to make Scrooge's a continued success. With all the money their uncle left you, you could have sold the store and turned into a social butterfly, spending your days playing tennis and planning charity benefits, but you didn't. Instead, you've expanded Scrooge's business and put it on the World Wide Web."

Eleanor harrumphed. "Playing tennis? What a boring way to spend one's life, and you know how I feel about charity of any kind."

"Yeah, I know. You've told me often enough."

She lifted her chin high. "There are plenty of jobs in this country for people who are willing to work. But *work* is the operative word here. If people aren't willing to work for their bread and butter, the rest of us shouldn't have to pay for their laziness. As far as I'm concerned, they can shut down all the do-gooder charity organizations."

"By the way, since we're talking about money and those who are willing to work, I was hoping you'd see fit to give me a raise. It's been two years since—"

She frowned, her palms flattening on the highly polished desktop. "A raise? I can't do that, Bob. If I gave you a raise, I'd have to give one to everyone. You're my accountant. Can you imagine what that would do to the bottom line?"

"But, El, I have expenses that—"

"You're just going to have to live within your means! If you hadn't had so many children—"

He stood, anger blanketing his face. "Those children are a gift from God. I wouldn't take—"

"A gift from God?" She let out a raucous laugh. "Then let God take care of them. If He gave them to you, it's His responsibility to help you provide for them. Not me!"

Disappointment showed on his face. "Come on, El, don't

talk that way. You know how important God is in my life. You need to—"

Ruthie pushed open the door, interrupting their conversation. "Mr. Kendall—that man from Imaginative Promotion—is here. You want me to show him in?"

Eleanor shot a quick glance Bob's way then answered. "Yes, give us sixty seconds then send him in."

Bob started for the door. "I thought I'd take off a bit early this afternoon. I was finally able to set up an appointment with Dr. Schopf. We're hopeful he'll be able to guide us to someone who can remove my daughter's port-wine stain birthmark."

"You can't leave early. I want you to work this evening. I need you to go over some projections with me, and tonight's the only time I can work them in. You'll have to do it another time." Eleanor began perusing the papers Ruthie had placed in the in-box on her desk. "I'm sorry, but business has to come first, Bob."

He headed for the door, muttering beneath his breath.

"Wait. Don't leave. I want you to sit in on this meeting with Mr. Kendall. I need your computer expertise."

He released a sigh of frustration then settled down in a nearby chair. "Guess I have no choice. You're the boss."

"Mrs. Scrooge. How nice to see you again." Mr. Kendall hurried into her office, briefcase in hand. "I think you're going to like our proposal for renovating your Web site. I can hardly wait to show it to you."

She gestured toward Bob. "You've met Robert Rachette, my chief accountant. He'll be sitting in on our discussion."

"Nice to see you again, Mr. Rachette." The man opened his briefcase, pulled out his laptop computer, and placed it on her desk. Lifting the lid, he pressed a button and the machine began to hum as it started up.

"You are going to be able to get our newly designed Web site up and running by October 1, aren't you?" Eleanor circled her desk and stood staring at the screen. "I've already purchased a heavy three-month advertising campaign to announce it, with full-page ads in the Sunday papers and daily ads on regional radio and television stations. I've done the surveys. I know what a good, easily navigated Web site can do for an already established business, and I want Scrooge's to ride that wave of success."

The man nodded and smiled confidently. "I've had my creative staff working on this for weeks. All we need is your approval to get started."

Ever the gentleman, Robert stood and pulled a chair up in front of the desk and gestured toward it. Eleanor gave him a nod then seated herself, crossing her ankles and folding her hands in her lap, her eyes focused on the computer screen. "So far, we've had some fairly good success selling our products on the Internet, but it's been a haphazard attempt with no real planning. I know by offering our fine-quality merchandise on the Internet in a tasteful, elegant, and easily maneuverable way, I can double our business the first year."

Mr. Kendall leaned forward and tapped the touchpad. Instantly the screen filled with color and a slide show began. "Watch this. We've tried to give your Web site a youthful, today appearance."

Eleanor let out a gasp. Rising quickly to her feet as several models on the screen danced their way down a runway with spotlights flashing in every direction and loud music as their background, she pointed at the monitor. "This is what you've done for me? I said I wanted elegance and class."

"This is the latest trend in Web sites. Most of—"

Furious, she turned away, her temper rising and spilling over. "I don't care what other Web sites are doing, Mr. Kendall. Scrooge's Department Store is not a follower. We're the leader. We set the trends. We don't listen to the dictates of others. Our new Web site needs to reflect us and what we have to offer to our clients. If they choose to do so, they can watch music videos on TV, not on our Web site. Turn that thing off. I refuse to spend my time watching—"

The man's face reddened. "You've only seen the flash introduction! You can't judge the entire Web site by seeing only the intro! At least you can take at look at the first page." He punched a key, and the first page appeared.

"That page is supposed to be better? I certainly don't like it. It does nothing for me. Nothing!" Willing herself to calm down, Eleanor took a deep breath and responded in a low, even voice, "Mr. Kendall, I would think that you, as the president of your company, would study the statistics. Don't you realize if you haven't captured a Web surfer with either your intro or your opening page, they won't bother to take a look at the rest of the Web site?" She gestured toward the screen. "In addition to its other flaws, not only is your presentation shoddy and cheap, the navigation is all wrong."

Mr. Kendall stared at her for a moment, as if trying to collect his thoughts. "I'm not sure you understand our purpose for doing it this way, Mrs. Scrooge." He motioned toward the tabs along the bottom of the screen. "Rather than use a navigation bar along the side or the top, we placed it at the bottom where there is room to display more selections. Your customers can always use the search feature to locate specific items. I think you'll find—"

"No! This is not acceptable. It's not at all what I want for Scrooge's!"

"Our other clients," the man said defensively, "have—"

"Don't tell me about your other clients! What they do is of no interest to me." Stepping back and crossing her arms, Eleanor frowned. "Do you think Scrooge's wants to be a carbon copy of your other clients? We are a unique business, Mr. Kendall. We cater to people who expect only the finest from us. I do not call what you are showing me *fine*! If this is the best you can come up with, then I'm afraid you're wasting both my time and yours."

Ignoring her comment, he tapped the computer's touchpad once again, and an entirely new screen came up. "Please, Mrs. Scrooge, take a look at this. Perhaps it's more to your liking. As you'll note, we've tried to keep the continuity of the entire Web site by using the same header but with a slightly different background color. The pricing—"

She rolled her eyes. Did the man not understand English? "Mr. Kendall, in the first place, I don't like your header. It does nothing to promote our image and our dedication to service. Those headers are cluttered. They spell cheap, and there's too much verbiage. Who is going to take time to read all of that garbage? Scrooge's isn't a discount house."

"I'm aware of that but—"

"We are a high-class operation, Mr. Kendall. That type of advertising would offend our customers. We have an excellent reputation in the upscale marketplace. One I'm proud of and have worked years to attain. I won't have it all thrown away by an inferior Web site."

With a look of frustration, Mr. Kendall turned to Robert. "It seems Mrs. Scrooge values your opinion, Mr. Rachette. What do you think?"

Just as she was sure he would, Robert lifted his hands with a slight grin and a shrug then nodded toward her. "She's the boss. You'll have to talk to her."

Eleanor couldn't resist a smile. Sweet, dependable, loyal Robert. He rarely disagreed with her. At least, Mr. Kendall was right about one thing. She did value Robert's opinion, though she seldom asked for it. "I'm sorry, Mr. Kendall, apparently your agency isn't qualified to do the kind of Web site we need for Scrooge's." She motioned toward the door. "Now if you'll excuse me, I have work to do."

The man narrowed his eyes, his face reddening even more. "My agency has put a lot of work into this project, Mrs.

Scrooge. We had hoped to—"

"I had only asked you to prepare a proposal, which was nothing more than giving you a chance to show me, without any obligation on my part, what your company could do for us. To be quite honest, Mr. Kendall, I expected better from you. I can see now I was wrong."

"Maybe we can rework it some. Tweak it up a bit here and there. Eliminate some of the clutter, as you call it. Perhaps a more—"

Enough was enough. "Mr. Kendall, that Web site needs more than a rework and a tweaking. You'd be much better off hitting the delete button and ridding yourself of the whole thing. That is, unless you can find a discount chain somewhere that might be interested. As Robert and my other employees can attest, I'm not well-known for giving second chances. I do the best I can, and I expect my employees and associates to do the same thing." She gestured toward his open laptop. "I suggest you take your computer and go. My mind is made up. Scrooge's won't be utilizing your company's services."

He glared at her with disgust as he slammed the laptop shut.

Eleanor moved around the desk and seated herself in the elegantly upholstered chair, folding her hands in her lap. "Robert, would you please show Mr. Kendall to the door?" She gave her head a slight shake as she watched the two men walk across the thick green carpet. She'd been so sure she'd chosen the right company to design the new Web site, but what Mr. Kendall had shown her was ridiculous, and nothing at all like what she'd explained she'd wanted. It was obvious they'd ignored her specifications.

"You did agree with me, didn't you?" she asked as Robert walked back across the room to retrieve the papers he'd brought in earlier.

He nodded. "One hundred percent."

Eleanor stood and began pacing about the room. "I wanted

something simple, but elegant. Colorful, yet tasteful. I even did a few sketches to show them what I had in mind."

"I thought your sketches were quite clear."

She stopped pacing and stood staring out the window. "I promised Everett on his deathbed that I would take Scrooge's to new heights. Haven't I done that?"

Robert nodded. "I would say so. You've done wonders for this business. Everett would be proud of you."

She turned, and for a brief moment, felt like that same little girl who always needed her best friend's approval for her sometimes unorthodox behavior. "It hasn't always been easy."

"I know, but you've weathered every storm quite capably."

"I do my best."

The corners of his mouth turned up slightly. "You always have."

"Do you think I'm too demanding? That I'm being unreasonable when I force my high standards on others?"

His slight grin broadened. "At times."

She digested his words carefully. "I have to be tough, Bobby." She paused, surprised she had called him by that childhood name. "I have a lot of responsibility riding on my shoulders. Think how many employees depend on Scrooge's for their livelihood. Being the owner and CEO of this corporation is an awesome responsibility. Competition is fierce. We have to be constantly moving forward, or we won't make it. The retail business is nothing like it was when Everett was running things."

"Scrooge's is in good hands. You're one of the most intelligent, capable women in this industry."

"Obviously I chose the wrong promotional firm, and now I doubt we'll have the new Web site ready by October first."

Seating herself again, she leaned back in her chair, her fingers again massaging her temples. "I had great expectations about Mr. Kendall's proposal. Now I'll have to start all over again and find another company. I still can't believe the substandard Web site he tried to sell me. It looked like amateurs created it."

"Even I, with as little knowledge as I have, could have done a better job than that."

Surprised by his words, Eleanor lowered her hands. "What do you know about building Web sites?"

⁂

Robert flinched at her question. Why had he blurted that out? What was he thinking? Knowing El, she'd keep at him until she got an answer that satisfied her.

She rose, circled her desk, and came to stand directly in front of him, her arms linked loosely across her chest. "I asked you a question."

Now I've done it. I have to tell her the truth. As a Christian, I can't lie about it. "I've always been fascinated by the Web. You know how I love computers and anything to do with them."

"That's your answer?" She tilted her head slightly and gazed at him. "Why do I get the impression you're keeping something from me?"

He pasted on a plastic smile and shrugged.

"You made a statement, Robert. You said even you could have done a better job than Mr. Kendall's company. What did you mean by that?"

two

She tapped the tip of her spike-heeled shoe impatiently. "I'm waiting."

Robert glanced at his watch. "I thought you said you had some work to do."

"You're avoiding my question, Robert Rachette."

He lifted both hands in surrender. "Okay, you win. I didn't want to tell you, but I've been working at a second job for the past two years. I know how you frown on your employees holding second jobs, but with all the expenses I've had since my wife died, I've had no other choice."

She gave him a haughty look. "My employees can't be at their best unless they give their full, undivided attention to working for me. That includes you, Robert. You're responsible for all the money that goes through Scrooge's. You need to be on your toes and have a clear head. The idea of you taking on a second job is ludicrous."

He hung his head. "You're reacting exactly as I knew you would. That's why I didn't want to tell you."

"You should have come to me before doing something as foolish as taking on a second job."

"I did come to you! Several times, and each time I asked you for a raise I got the same answer you gave me today: No! I was desperate, El. I have a family to support. My mom is no longer physically able to help with the children. My family's financial needs increase every year, yet other than the blanket cost of living increase we all got three years ago, I haven't had an actual raise in nearly six years."

She fidgeted with the diamond brooch on her designer suit. "I—I hadn't realized it'd been that long."

"You and I have been friends as long as I can remember. You promoted me to assistant of accounting at Scrooge's after Everett died, knowing I was nothing more than a lowly accountant without a CPA certification. Six years ago, you made me head of the accounting department and gave me a twenty percent raise. That's the last one I've had."

Eleanor started to say something but pursed her lips together instead, her gaze still pinned on him. He wished he knew what was going through her mind at that moment, but she was a master at keeping her true feelings hidden, a trick she'd told him she'd learned when her father would find her and beat her.

"I hate to say this—it makes me sound ungrateful—but I've considered leaving Scrooge's and finding work elsewhere."

Eleanor reared back, her eyes rounded in surprise. "You'd leave me? After all I've done for you?"

Robert paused, giving deep thought before responding. He certainly didn't want to be fired, but he had to stand his ground. He'd let her dominate him for far too long. "The way I see it, our business relationship is a two-way thing, El. Yes, you gave me the opportunity to advance, despite my lack of being a Certified Public Account, but I've done a good job here. Like you, I've put my all into my work. I've never shirked my duties. In fact, I've gone way beyond what you've asked of me. But there comes a time when a man has to evaluate where he is and what he's doing. I have to think about my future and the future of my children. They are such good kids, and they ask so little of me. I want to be able to do things for them. Maybe, one day, send them off to college for the education you and I never had."

"But you and I have done all right, haven't we?"

"Let's face it, El. If it weren't for old Everett Scrooge falling in love with you and asking you to marry him, probably neither one of us would still be working here."

For only a brief moment, Eleanor seemed to smart at his words, and then she brightened, recovering like she always did when an impossible problem needed solving. "Enough of this kind of talk. You are not leaving me, Robert Rachette. You and I are a team. We've always been a team."

He gave her a teasing smirk. "Yeah, you're the head coach, and I'm the water boy."

A smile curled at her bright red lips. "You know that's not true. You're a very important part of my business life. Now, tell me about this other job of yours. Exactly what do you do?"

Though she seemed genuinely interested, he still felt uncomfortable talking about it. He'd been so sure she'd fire him if she learned he had been moonlighting. "A few years ago I decided I would do everything in my power to make sure my precious daughter would get the medical attention she deserved," he began, watching her carefully while trying to decide how much he should say. "I noted the Internet was beginning to burgeon with Web sites, both commercial and private. I purchased a used computer so I could work at home and began learning the HTML computer language, with the idea that I might be able to work at home evenings and weekends, creating and maintaining Web sites. Cal Bender, one of the men at my church, owns a small Web hosting business. When I confided in him what I was doing and how I really needed to find a way to subsidize my income, he hired me. Since I've always had a great interest in the Internet and have used it to research my daughter's birthmark, I was already pretty Web site savvy, so it didn't take long for me to catch on to his company's way of doing things."

Her balled fist went to her hip. "Why didn't you tell me

this before? You knew I was planning to revamp and enlarge Scrooge's Web site. I could have used your input!"

"Because I knew you'd be upset if you found out I was working outside of Scrooge's, that's why. I sure didn't want to invite the possibility of getting fired!"

Eleanor proceeded as if she hadn't heard a word he'd said about getting fired. "Is any of your work up on the Internet?"

He nodded, still hesitant to reveal too much about his part-time job. He, better than anyone else who worked for her, knew how quickly she could be angered into doing something rash. And, like she'd told Mr. Kendall, she was not known for giving second chances.

She took him by the hand and pulled him toward the computer on her desk. "Show me."

"Remember? You said you had work to do. I don't want to keep you from something important."

"At this point, nothing is more important to me than getting the new Web site up before my October 1 deadline." She moved to one side and gestured toward the chair.

Knowing arguing with her was futile, he sat down and typed in the URL address for the most recent Web site he'd designed and completed. "This one is for a tool and die company. Not very glamorous, I'm afraid."

Eleanor leaned over his shoulder and stared at the screen. "You did that?"

Robert flinched. *Oh no! Here comes her criticism.* Although quite proud of the Web site, he felt as though he'd laid himself bare by letting her see it.

She leaned even closer, scrutinizing the screen with an intensity that unnerved him. Then, smiling up at him, she said, "It's wonderful, Robert. Clean lines. No wasted words. Easy navigation. That's what I wanted for our Web site."

Floored by her compliment, he allowed himself to smile.

Maybe he could risk talking about it. "See over here on the left side? I've added links to the various sections. It took me weeks to catalog thousands of parts, but now a customer from anywhere in the world can order as many or as few parts as they need from this Web site and have them shipped overnight. For their business, being user-friendly and having their customers able to find exactly what they needed with a touch of a finger was their number one priority. Yet they wanted their site to spell quality."

Eleanor maneuvered herself up closer and scrolled to the shopping cart icon at the top right corner of the page. Instantly, a detailed but well organized order sheet appeared. Her eyes widened. "Robert, this is so much better than anything Mr. Kendall had to offer. I must say I'm impressed!"

His emotions feeling somewhat mixed, Robert watched silently while she moved through several more pages. El was famous for her left-handed compliments. They always seemed to end with a "Yes, but. . ." Though she praised something, she always added a criticism or suggestion to make it better. She could never leave well enough alone or admit someone's idea or work needed no improvement.

Finally returning to the home page, she looked up at him, a glint in her eye. "You must do our Web site."

After taking a moment to recover, Robert stared at her, astounded that she would even consider such a thing. He pointed at El. "You," he said, pausing for emphasis, "want me"—he pulled his hand back and tapped the end of his finger on his chest—"to do Scrooge's Web site?"

Her brows lifted as she gave a ladylike shrug. "Why not?" The question rolled off her tongue as easily as if she were asking if he wanted cream in his coffee. "You already work for Scrooge's, Robert. You'd be the perfect one to do it. From the looks of this Web site, you certainly have the know-how.

Besides, I'd be right here by your side to give you my input."

That's one of the reasons I wouldn't want to do it, even if I were qualified. Having you breathing down my neck would make me a nervous wreck. "Look, El, I know you were disappointed with the proposal Mr. Kendall gave you, but I'm sure there are dozens of other companies out there who are more than capable of doing an excellent job. You need to talk to one of them."

"But I want you to do it!"

"I'm a number cruncher, El. Doing an Internet catalog for a parts company is a far cry from doing a high-fashion, upscale department store Web site like Scrooge's."

Eleanor cupped her fingers around his wrist and lifted her beautiful, clear blue eyes. "At least give it a try."

He gave his head a slight shake and tried to pull away. This was the same technique she'd used when they were kids. All she'd had to do was place her tiny hand on his wrist and lift her big blue eyes to his, and he'd melt. And the sad thing was—she knew it. He could never refuse little El, and that weakness had gotten him in trouble many times. "I couldn't do it justice, El. Besides, I have my own work to do."

"But you have time to work a part-time job?"

Frustrated, he shook his head. "No, El, I don't have time to work a part-time job, but I have to work it so I can make ends meet. There's a big difference. Thanks to my friend who owns the hosting business, most of the time I can work my part-time job from home where I can be near my children and not have to hire a baby-sitter. That job is a godsend."

He could almost hear the gears in her brain turning as Eleanor gazed into his eyes. Expecting she would drop her idea was pure fantasy. Once Eleanor made up her mind about something, nothing could make her change it.

"What if. . ." She tilted her head coyly, the same way

he'd seen her do when she'd first caught the attention of Everett Scrooge. Eleanor was a master at using her feminine wiles, after all else failed, to get her way. "What if I paid you whatever that hosting company is paying you? Would you do it then?"

"In addition to my regular salary?" He wanted to kick himself the minute the question had come out of his mouth. He knew he'd opened the door for something that could be a real pain. Pleasing Eleanor Scrooge was nearly impossible. Ask any employee.

"Well, I was going to have to pay Mr. Kendall's company."

Robert decided to play her at her own game. "And you're going to pay me whatever you would have had to pay him?" He could tell she was uncomfortable by his question. He could see it in her eyes, and he had to stifle a smile. He rarely offered Eleanor a challenge, and it felt good.

"You already work for me, Robert. Since you'll be working in addition to your regular forty-hour week, I'll have to pay you at the overtime rate. Surely you don't expect more."

Determined not to let her have her way and talk him into something he didn't want to do or feel qualified to do, once again, he tried to pull away, but her fingers held fast. "Look, I'm already committed to Cal. He hired me and took a chance on me when I really needed a part-time job, then spent many hours teaching me the things he knew and had learned the hard way. I owe him, El. I can't just walk out on him. He's depending on me."

"You owe me, too, Bobby."

He hated it when she batted those long eyelashes at him. *There she goes, using that persuasive, childlike tone of voice on me—the one I could never refuse.* "Believe me; I appreciate all you've done for me. I know I could never have advanced to the position I've attained with Scrooge's without your help, and—"

"I didn't just help you get that position, Bobby. I'm the one who put you there. I'd hoped I wouldn't have to remind you. Promoting you was the first thing I did when I inherited this business, or have you forgotten?"

"I remember, El." Robert swallowed at the lump in his throat. She was right. Her words were true. If El hadn't vowed to repay him for saving her life when they were children, he'd probably be working at some dead-end job for minimum wage. Though he wanted to provide for his family in the best possible way, he'd never been confident in his capabilities, preferring to stay in the background and letting others take credit for his work. "I'll be forever grateful to you. But, El, you have to remember—I have access to all of Scrooge's financial information. I know what the other employees make, especially those who are on commission. The amount of responsibility I carry with this company doesn't begin to match the wages I'm paid."

"You're a salaried person, Robert. Salaried persons rarely make as much as a commissioned salesperson. You know that."

How many times had she offered that excuse when he asked for a raise in pay? "I do know that, El, but it doesn't seem fair. Though I've never talked to anyone at another company in the same type of position, I'm reasonably sure they make far more money than I do."

She lifted her chin proudly, an indication she was about to counter his statement with an irrefutable answer. "I operate Scrooge's as frugally as possible. I admit that. But to be competitive in this day and age, especially with the advent of the Internet, I have to keep operating expenses to a bare minimum. Surely you, who, as you've said, has access to those records, can see that. Even though our profits have risen considerably since I took over the helm, so have our expenses."

Robert clamped his fingers over her hand and pulled it

from his wrist then stepped away, needing to put some space between them, away from those pleading blue eyes. "I'm sorry, El. You'll have to find someone else. I don't have the time or the talent to build your Web site."

Eleanor stared up at him, her jaw set in a way that told him he was losing the battle. "Robert," she said slowly, her gaze pinned on his. "I hate to do this, but you give me no choice."

Panic seized his heart. Surely she wouldn't fire him for refusing to build a Web site, would she? Eleanor was impulsive, no doubt about it, but she was also one of the most business-savvy women he'd ever heard of. Though her personal life had been one of complete chaos, she had a head for business that would put many CEOs to shame.

Her eyes narrowed menacingly. "You are going to build Scrooge's Web site, Robert. As your employer, I'm ordering you to do it."

Even though she had threatened to fire him if he refused to build the Web site, surely she wouldn't do it. How long would it take him to find another job? He doubted Cal would need him on a full-time basis. Not yet, anyway. And what company would want to hire him when they found out Eleanor Scrooge had fired him?

Her hands went to her hips. "Did you hear me, Robert?"

He stared at her in disbelief, not sure what to say or how to react. He'd called her bluff, and she'd met it head-on. "I—I heard you, El," he answered meekly, his heart racing.

"I'm asking you point-blank, and I expect a direct answer. Are you going to obey my orders, or am I going to have to fire you?"

"I can't, El. I'm not—"

"No more excuses. I want an answer."

He sucked in a deep breath. Why couldn't she see it? He wasn't qualified to build the kind of high-quality Web site she wanted. If she were unhappy with him for refusing to do it, he could only imagine how upset she would be if he produced a product she considered inferior. "I'm sorry, El. I'd like to do what you ask, but I can't."

She wagged a finger in his face. "By refusing to obey my orders you're forcing me to fire you. You do realize that, don't you? I cannot allow insubordination. Are you saying you refuse to build the Scrooge Web site?"

Robert clutched the edge of the desk. "Please don't do this to me. You know I'd never refuse you anything, but the Web sites I've worked on so far have been simple compared to what you're asking me to do. Why can't you understand that?"

Obviously upset, Eleanor glared at him, her piercing eyes skillfully scanning his face. "Why can't you understand what I'm saying? I know you, Robert Rachette. You never give anything less than your best. Apparently, I have more confidence in your abilities than you do."

"I appreciate your faith in me, but I'm—"

"Try it, Robert, please. For me?"

Her voice fairly dripped with sweetness, and he felt like he was eight years old again. He hated it when she did that. "Okay, you win. I'll try," he conceded, giving his head a shake of defeat, "but don't expect too much."

Pulling a thick file folder from her desk drawer and reaching it toward him, Eleanor beamed with a smile of victory. "Your best is all I ask."

He frowned and took the folder. "What's this?"

"The same information I put together for Mr. Kendall. You'll be needing it."

Opening the folder, he flipped through a few pages, finding the instructions she'd given Mr. Kendall were nothing like the Web site he'd presented to her. No wonder she was furious. "You really expect me to have Scrooge's new Web site up and running by the first of October? That doesn't give me much time. I can't possibly keep up with my regular job and work on that, too."

"Your assistant can help you."

"You've got an answer for everything, haven't you?"

"It's my job to come up with answers." She smiled broadly. "Now go to your office and get busy. You need to get started on it today."

Robert felt himself bristle. Hadn't he already told her he planned to leave early to take Ginny to the doctor? "I can't."

"Oh, that's right. You mentioned you have some kind of doctor appointment. But this is important, Robert. That appointment will have to wait. You need to get on this as soon as possible."

Saddened by her lack of concern, he closed the file and folded his hands over it. "I know the Web site is important, El, but so is my daughter. I'm not going to miss this doctor's appointment. I'll start work on the Web site the first thing in the morning."

She waved him toward the door. "Oh, all right. Take your daughter to the doctor if you must, but it seems to me something like that could be put off for a few weeks. She was born with that birthmark. What difference would a delay make?"

"I guess you'd have to be a parent to understand." His heart grew heavier with each step as he trudged across the thick pile of the carpet and took hold of the doorknob. *Why do I always give in to El?*

three

Robert sat in Dr. Schopf's office, holding nearly ten-year-old Ginny on his lap, his protective arms wrapped securely around her, his heart wrenching as he stared at the bright red birthmark on her cheek. *God, I'll never understand why You allowed this beautiful, innocent child to be born with a horrible port-wine stain birthmark on her sweet face.*

Dr. Schopf pulled his stool up close and squinted at her face, his hand cupping her chin. "My associate and I have conferred on this, Mr. Rachette, and we agree that most of the color can be removed quite successfully with laser therapy. And, since someday soon she will more than likely begin to wear makeup, there is a good chance her birthmark may be nearly unnoticeable. But it can't be done overnight. It will probably take a number of treatments."

Though somewhat excited by Dr. Schopf's words, Bob felt his heart plummet. "How many treatments?"

Dr. Schopf paused, eyeing first Ginny then Bob. "As many as it takes. We can never say for sure. There are too many variables. I would say Ginny's port-wine stain, or PWS as we call it, is a grade one, which is the least invasive. She has good, what we call, peek-through skin. That type of stain is very responsive to therapy and doesn't usually form cobblestones."

Bob felt his breath catch in his throat. "Cobblestones? I've read about them while researching on the Internet."

The doctor bobbed his head toward the girl. "Lesions with deeper vessel involvement often form cobbling as the lesion ages, but I doubt that will happen with Ginny. Laser therapy is ideal for her, and the earlier a child has this treatment, the better."

"That's good news." Though a sigh of relief escaped Bob's lips, there was so much more he wanted to know. "What about risks or side effects associated with the therapy?"

"This type of therapy is quite safe, especially since her PWS is on her cheek and away from her eye, her nose, and not too near her mouth. Though the treatments aren't pleasant, they are tolerable by using an analgesic cream first. Each of the zaps she'll experience will feel much like a bad rubber band snap and only last a second. I'm sure those who administer her treatments will do everything they can to keep your daughter as comfortable as possible. After each treatment, there will be a slight swelling and redness in the area, and possibly a mottled appearance will occur. A gray color may persist for approximately three to seven days, but this slowly resolves itself. After that, improvement in the overall color is expected. I'm sure she's as anxious to rid her lovely little face of that stain as you are."

"*They'll* keep her comfortable? You can't do the treatment?"

He shook his head. "No. Laser therapy takes special training and equipment. There are a number of fine hospitals that specialize in laser therapy. I would highly recommend the Arkansas Children's Hospital in Little Rock. They have a fine reputation."

"Little Rock? That's nearly fifteen hundred miles from here! I could never afford to take her that far away. I—I was hoping it could be done—closer."

"Cincinnati also has a fine laser therapy program. It's not quite nine hundred miles," the doctor offered, rubbing his chin thoughtfully.

Bob's grip tightened about his precious child. "My insurance may cover the treatment, but I doubt it will cover the costs of the trips and hotel to either Cincinnati or Little Rock. I could try to get a loan—"

The kindly doctor placed a consoling hand on Bob's arm. "I don't want to get your hopes up, Mr. Rachette. Most insurance companies refuse to pay for this sort of treatment since they claim it is done for cosmetic purposes only."

Bob's righteous indignation kicked in. "Cosmetic purposes? Removing a port-wine stain from a child's face? That makes no sense at all!"

Dr. Schopf shrugged. "I agree. All I can do is recommend that you present a good argument to your insurance company then pray they'll accept your claim. I hate to be the bearer of bad news, but I've heard of very few patients whose insurance company was in the least bit cooperative."

Bob nudged Ginny off his lap and rose slowly, his heart aching as he extended his hand. "Thanks, Dr. Schopf, but from the sound of things, Ginny's treatments may have to be put off for a long time. My wife died two years ago. I'm a single father with a large family to support. The kind of money we're talking about is way beyond my reach. I guess this trip to your office has been in vain. I'm sorry to have taken up your time."

Dr. Schopf tousled Ginny's curls then grasped Bob's hand with a hearty shake. "If there is anything I can do to try to convince your insurance company this is a legitimate claim, I'll be happy to do it."

"Isn't the doctor going to take this red thing off my face, Daddy?" Ginny asked, looking glum and grabbing her father's hand as they exited the office.

Blinking hard, he sent her the best smile he could muster. "Not now, honey. Maybe in a year or two."

"But I thought—"

"So did I, sweetheart. But I guess the Lord didn't think this was the best time. We have to leave it in His hands, okay?" The disappointed look on his daughter's face ripped at his heart, but he tried not to show it. "How about some chocolate chip ice cream?"

Ginny lifted her watery gaze to his, her lower lip trembling. "I'm not hungry for ice cream, Daddy. Can we just go home?"

ès

Engrossed on the project in which she was working, Eleanor barely looked up from her computer when Robert entered her office the next morning.

"You're in early." He moved to the coffeepot on the credenza and poured himself a cup. "Want one?"

She gave him a look of veiled disgust. "I'm always in early. Not all of us can keep banker's hours. I'd hoped you be in much earlier."

"Little touchy this morning?" He hastily added a smile, hoping his quick response hadn't upset her. Though she was a fairly good sport, she never appreciated jokes or careless repartee at her expense. "It's even seven o'clock yet, El. Bad night? Did you have one of your headaches?"

"Actually, I had a very good night, what there was of it. I couldn't sleep for thinking about the Web site." She brightened, as if just the thought of it gave her new energy. "I'm so anxious to get started on it. I thought we could—"

He held up a palm between them and shook his head. "Not so fast. There are a number of major preliminary things that have to be accomplished before we get started. Important things."

Eleanor clicked an icon on her computer screen and pushed the keyboard toward the monitor, turning to him with her undivided attention. "Like what? I thought we could get started on the content today."

Bob pulled a chair up in front of her desk, took a few papers from his briefcase, and sat down, leaning forward. "For one, I have to bring Tom, my assistant up to speed. We can't let the accounting department get behind just because we need to get the Web site up and running. My department is my first and most important priority." He raised his brows. "Okay?"

Eleanor rolled her eyes. "Yes, I suppose so. How long do you think that will take?"

"Tom's a good man and catches on fast. He's already familiar with most of the procedures. But you have to understand, El, right up front: If I'm needed in the accounting department, this Web site project is going to have to be put on hold. We sure don't want any foul-ups happening in the financial end of your business."

Her eyes widened. "We can't get started today?"

He reached across the desk and patted her hand. "*We* can't get started on it today, but you can. I want you to set aside as much time as you can, feed the words—fashions, department stores, designers, boutiques, and any other words you can think of that would describe finer women's fashions, into your computer—into the search engine. That should bring up hundreds of Web sites. I want you to check them out and bookmark any that catch your eye or give you ideas you might want to incorporate on Scrooge's Web site. Especially pay attention to their navigation designs. I also need you to make out a list of all the features you'd like to put on our Web site. Watch for colors that appeal to you, graphics, flash intros—"

Eleanor screwed up her face. "Flash intro? Somehow that conjures up an image of a scruffy old man in a raincoat."

Robert leaned back in his chair with a laugh. "Not that kind of flash. Flash intros are quite often used as the very first page on a Web site. The first thing a customer or client will see when they type in Scrooge's dot com. They're catchy, quick, and usually have moving graphics. If done right, they're quite effective in presenting the overall image you want your site to convey in only a few seconds of time. I really think we should use one for Scrooge's."

"I don't want anything like the beginning of Mr. Kendall's presentation."

He nodded. "I know. A good, classy flash intro will give your customers an instant impression of what the Web site is about. Uniqueness, innovativeness, quality, and good service."

Eleanor's face lit up. "That's exactly what I want, Bob! And to think I was even considering Mr. Kendall's company when you were right here under my nose all this time."

"His company's Web site designers are pros, El. I'm not. I'm not even in the same league."

"But don't you see? You and I think alike. You know what I want." She rose and circled the desk, enthusiasm illuminating her lovely face. "They didn't have a clue, even though I thoroughly explained my wishes to Mr. Kendall before they even started. You know me, Bob, sometimes even better than I know myself."

Her statement made him laugh and brought back old memories of the little girl he'd grown up with. Little El. How she'd changed from that first day she and her family moved into the run-down trailer house down the street from his parents' home. Even though she had to wear her sister Eileen's secondhand clothes and she had come to school with nothing more than peanut butter and crackers in her lunch sack, there'd always been something special about her. Yes, he did know El better than anyone else knew her. They'd been pals and cohorts most of their lives. Though he'd never told anyone, not even his mother, he'd been in love with El since the time they'd been in the fourth grade and he'd beat the school bully up for making wisecracks about her. El had hugged and kissed him that day, and he'd never been the same.

He'd always been her protector. Though she'd dated many boys during their high school years, none of them had been able to win her heart. At least a dozen suitors had asked to escort her to their senior prom, but she'd turned them all down, saying she wanted to attend that special occasion with her best friend. How proud he'd been that night, dressed in his rental tuxedo. Since his mother had made the elegant, red satin dress for El, she had come to their home that evening to get ready, and his mother helped her with her hair. He still had the snapshot his father had taken of the two of them as he'd pinned the delicate white orchid to her shoulder. Though he'd never actually told her how much he loved her, he had always planned to ask her to marry him as soon as he graduated and got a job. But that was not to be. The day of their high school graduation, El announced she was leaving for New York City where she planned to get a job in a big fashion house.

"Bob? Did you hear me?"

He shook his head to clear his thoughts and gave her a shy grin. "Yeah, I heard you."

Moving back around the desk, she gracefully seated herself before smoothing at her hair. "You and I have always been a good team, haven't we?"

"I've always thought so."

She lowered her head a bit and batted her long, dark lashes. "When I was a little girl, I used to drape a scarf over my head and pretend the two of us were getting married. Isn't that funny?"

Her words startled him. "Would that have been so bad?"

"Marrying you? No, of course not. But you never loved me. You married Lydia."

"You went to New York. Life went on. I met Lydia and fell in love with her. The rest is history."

"If—if you hadn't met Lydia—"

"You wouldn't have married me, El. We both know that. You wanted to make your mark in the world. You set a goal for yourself, and you went after it."

"I might have married you, if you'd waited for me."

"I could never have offered you what old Mr. Scrooge did. You're an elegant woman, El, with elegant tastes. I'll never be more than an accountant." He gave her a weak smile. "And a part-time Webmaster, thanks to you firing Mr. Kendall. Lydia and I had a good life. I loved that woman, and I love each of the children we had together." Bob rose and tossed the papers onto her desk. "You might look these over when you get a chance."

El was silent for a moment then asked, "Could you have loved me as much as you loved Lydia?"

"I've always loved you, El. I probably always will."

"But not in the same way you loved her?"

He moved slowly toward the door. "Hard to say. You never gave me a chance."

"How did your doctor's appointment come out yesterday?"

He turned slowly, surprised she had even remembered it. "It turned out to be the old good news, bad news type of thing. The good news is that Ginny is a perfect candidate for laser therapy. Her birthmark is pretty much on the surface."

"I'd think you'd be happy about that. Isn't that what you wanted to hear?"

"Yes, but then I found out that insurance companies won't pay for the removal of port-wine stain lesions."

"Why? That doesn't make any sense!"

He swallowed at the lump in his throat. "They consider it elective cosmetic surgery."

"Surely you have some savings. Couldn't you pay for it?"

He wanted to shake her. "Savings? On what I make at Scrooge's? There are no savings, El. It takes my entire salary just to keep our monthly bills paid. That's why I have a second job. Do you have any idea what it takes to meet the needs of a family of six?"

"You and Lydia should have thought of that before you had all those children."

He sucked in a deep breath of air and counted to ten. "Each of our children was a gift from God. We were doing fine until Lydia got sick and had to give up her part-time job, but with all the extra expenses of having to hire someone to come in and care for her, plus the extra for child care, and the deductible on my insurance, not to mention the funeral expenses—"

"I'm sorry, Bob. I didn't mean to upset you. But, it seems to me, the expense of having all those children and having to provide for them is the very reason you are having trouble making it on your salary. Maybe your daughter could just put some makeup on that little birthmark of hers."

His fists clenched at his sides. "Are you so caught up in your own life and your own little world, you have no idea what is going on in other people's lives, or even care? That birthmark is not an insignificant little thing that can be covered up with a dab of makeup. If you would have come to our home any one of those dozens of times we invited you, you would know that her port-wine stain birthmark is about two inches long and three-quarters of an inch wide, and it is as brilliant as that red satin dress my mother made for you when you were voted prom queen. Ginny's been teased and ridiculed about it by her peers, and she's had adults go out of their way to take a look at it. She hates that birthmark. So do I. I'll guarantee you, if you had been born with a birthmark just half that big, you would have robbed a bank to get the money to have it removed!"

She tilted her chin indignantly. "You needn't bark at me because of it. Your God is the one who allowed it to happen."

"I'm well aware my family's welfare is of no concern to you but someday—even though I have no idea how—I'm going to see to it that my child gets rid of that awful thing. I don't want her to have to go through her high school years feeling like she is a freak. And don't talk to me of what God would do. You've made it perfectly clear you have no use for God in your life. How would you know what God would or would not allow?"

Her hands went to her hips. "What did God ever do for me? Where was He when my father was beating me? Beating my mother? Or beating Eileen? If He were real, He should have stepped in and protected me. I'm a good person. I've worked hard to get where I am. I've done all of this by myself. It's about time I get the recognition I deserve!"

"It's about time you grew up, El, that's what. The world does not revolve around you and your business. Some of the rest of us actually have a life. You'd do well to get one for yourself." He whirled around and moved quickly through the door, slamming it behind him, nearly knocking the coffee cup from Ruthie's hand as she stood outside the door.

Ruthie snickered. "Were you actually hollering at our royal highness? I could hear you clear out in the hall."

Bob felt a flush rise to his cheeks. "She always knows how to push my buttons. Sorry."

Ruthie placed her cup on her desk then sat down, a smile playing at her lips. "You're the only one I know who would dare stand up to that woman."

"Yeah, and I think my big mouth may have just cost me my job."

four

Bob stared at the computer screen as he sat at his desk shortly after noon, munching on the last bite of the ham and cheese sandwich his oldest daughter had packed for his lunch. *Oh, El, what have you dragged me into? Building the kind of Web site you want is going to be a monumental job. I'm not at all sure I'm capable of undertaking such a large project.*

He startled when the phone rang and grabbed it up quickly, half expecting to hear El's angry voice.

"Her highness wants you in her office immediately." It was Ruthie.

"Does that mean I still have a job, or does she want me to come in so she can fire me in person?"

A giggle sounded in his ear. "You tell me. You know her better than I do."

"Pray for me, Ruthie. I need this job."

Two minutes later, after grinning back at Ruthie's reassuring smile of encouragement, he passed her desk and entered Eleanor's office.

She motioned him toward the chair then sat staring icily at him for a long moment before speaking. "I'm going to ignore that little outburst of yours and pretend it never happened," she said coolly.

"I—I spoke out of turn. I'm sorry, but I meant what I said, El." His heart pounded. "My family means everything to me. I refuse to have anyone, even you, ridicule me for having them."

The silence in the room was overwhelming.

"I'm sorry for being so judgmental," Eleanor finally said. "What you do with your personal life and how you spend your money is your business. I have no right to interfere."

"You're special to me, El. You always have been and you always will be. I care about you."

"I care about you, too." She gave him a shy grin, dipping her head slightly. "I've never told you, but when that invitation to your wedding arrived at my dingy little New York apartment, I sat down and cried."

Bob felt his eyes widen at her unexpected statement. "Cried? Why?"

"I—I always thought—someday—the two of us—"

"Two of us would what?"

"I know it was silly to have such feelings. After all, I'm the one who left for New York, never planning to return to Newport, but I always felt you were mine and that you'd always wait for me—in case I ever decided to get married and settle down. I never dreamed you would meet and marry Lydia."

Awed, Bob floundered for words. "You actually—uh—thought—"

"About marrying you? Spending the rest of my life as your wife? Oh, yes. You're the only man I've ever truly loved, but I wanted big city life—a successful career. I couldn't stay in Newport, and you had no desire to leave. I—I wasn't cut out to be a small town wife. I wanted bright lights, designer clothing, and expensive jewelry!"

He let out a pent-up sigh. "And I could never have given you any of those."

Eleanor rose and moved gracefully around her desk, placing her hand on his shoulder. "No, you couldn't give me any of those things, but you could have given me the one thing I've craved, needed most, never had, or been able to buy."

Bob frowned, confused by her words. "What's that?

"Love. Unselfish, sacrificing, enduring love. It's the one thing that has eluded me all my life. How I envied Lydia."

"You never told me!"

She gave his shoulder a tender pat. "I know. And by the time I was forced to let go of my dream and come back to Newport, hoping you and I could get together, you were married to Lydia."

Bob found himself speechless. El had actually loved him? It was all too much to comprehend.

"She was the fine, upstanding Christian woman you deserved. From what you said, a Bible-believing, God-fearing woman. I was, and still am, nothing like her. She was the perfect match for you. Then, because you were good enough to help me get a job at Scrooge's, I met and married Everett Scrooge, and my life changed. Finally, I had the status and financial standing I've always craved. I loved him like a good friend, but never as a husband, and he knew it."

His heart went out to her. How little she knew of the real meaning of life. "You may have achieved those things, El, but you've missed so much. I had Lydia's love. I have my children and a God who loves me and died on the cross for me. I know I will spend eternity in heaven with Him because I have confessed my sins and accepted Him as my Savior."

She threw her head back with a harsh laugh. "You? A sinner? That's a joke. Robert Rachette never did anything wrong in his life!"

"God's Word says all have sinned. That means me, you, everyone."

"I don't think of myself as a sinner."

"But you are a sinner, El. I'm not calling you a sinner. God is. He's the one who made the rules."

"Look at you! You're telling me you love a God who would put a terrible red birthmark on your daughter's face? And then not give you the money to have it removed? I don't want a God like that. Who would?"

"I may not have the material things that are important to you, but I'm rich and blessed beyond belief."

"Don't be too sure of that." She moved back to her tapestry upholstered desk chair and stood behind it, her hands cradled over its rounded back. "You've never tasted of the joys satisfaction, wealth, and renown can bring. It's a heady feeling of security like nothing else. For the first time in my life, I can have anything I want. Can you say that?"

"But not love. You said it yourself, El." Bob stared off in space, avoiding her accusing eyes. "No, I can't say that, but my God owns the cattle on a thousand hills, the wealth in every mine. As our loving Father, He gives us what is best for us."

"Oh? Does that mean He's going to pay for your daughter's treatments?"

God, give me the wisdom to answer El as You would have me answer. I want to be a witness for You. "I honestly don't know, El, but if it is His will that Ginny have that birthmark removed, He will provide a way to have it done. I have to trust Him."

As if uncomfortable with the direction in which their conversation was moving, Eleanor motioned toward the door. "You'd better get back to your office so you can wrap up things with your assistant. I'm expecting your full, undivided attention toward the creation of Scrooge's new Web site beginning tomorrow."

Relieved she hadn't called him in to fire him, Bob stood and smiled. "Be sure you have that list ready."

❧

"I'll have it ready." Eleanor watched as the lean, handsome man moved out the door of her office, closing it gently behind him. The years had been good to him. Though the cinnamon-colored hair at his temples was beginning to show signs of silver, and he'd been through more than most men have to go through in a lifetime, he still had the same boyish expression she remembered from their childhood. Little Bobby Rachette.

The best friend a girl could have.

Absentmindedly, she rotated the huge diamond ring on her left hand, barely noticing the faceted colors reflecting beneath the glow of her desk lamp. She'd been telling him the truth about envying Lydia, even though she was sure he hadn't believed her. What would her life have been like if she'd stayed in Newport, married Bobby, and settled down to raise the family she'd always known he wanted? Would she have been content to exist on a lowly accountant's salary? Live from paycheck to paycheck? He would have wanted children.

Would she have been a good mother? As good as Lydia? Or would she have resented Bob and the deprived life they would have shared? Maybe their marriage would have ended in divorce. She shuddered at the thought. Divorce! She hated that ugly word. How many times had her father threatened her mother with that word? Reminding her that his unemployment check and the money he sometimes won gambling were the only things that kept food on the table and a roof over their heads?

Food? Their food had amounted to only a few paltry staples, barely enough to satisfy their growling bellies. And a roof? Even that leaked. Why hadn't her mother realized there were other choices for them? Why hadn't she taken her and her sister to a shelter? Asked for help? Gone on welfare?

El smoothed at her designer suit then squared her shoulders and lifted her head. No, she'd made the right decision when she'd left Bob behind and moved to New York. Though she hadn't made her fortune there, she had experienced a different, sometimes satisfying lifestyle, and coming back to Newport when she did, had been perfect timing. She'd begun work at Scrooge's, met Everett Scrooge and married him, and now she was the sole owner of his home, his financial holdings, and his business. She was Mrs. Eleanor Scrooge, the envy of most of the women of Newport.

Facing her computer and opening up the document titled "Ideas for My New Web Site," she began to type. Tomorrow, she and Bob would begin putting together the new www.Scrooges.com Web site. Just the idea made her creative juices tingle.

The next two weeks went by rapidly. Both Bob and Eleanor worked from seven to seven daily. Many times, she watched him copy work over onto his speed drive before leaving his office so he could transfer the day's work over to his home computer and work on it that night. She was sure he was working until the wee hours of the morning, but he never complained.

❧

"I'm really pleased with the overall look of our Web site," Eleanor said one morning as they tried several different background color combinations.

Bob took his eyes off the computer screen long enough to look up at her. "But?"

She frowned. "But?"

He let his gaze go to the keyboard. "Usually when you give me a compliment, it's followed with a but—and then you tell me the way you think something could be improved."

Her index finger went contemplatively to her chin. "I was wondering if we shouldn't change the font. The one you're using is a bit too masculine."

"Do you want something more feminine, or do you want one that's easy to read?"

"I really like this one." She pointed at the list of fonts on the screen.

Without looking up, he gave his head a shake. "Too many curlicues and tails on the letters."

"What about this? It's a nice font," she said, pointing at another.

"Nope. Same thing. You have your choice between these two."

Eleanor leaned over his shoulder, grabbed hold of the mouse, and highlighted the word *Scrooge,* then selected another from the font menu. Instantly the plain word took on a unique, more feminine appearance. "How's this?" she asked sweetly, seeming pleased with herself.

"For the logo only?"

Smiling, she bobbed her head.

He twisted first one way and then the other, squinting at the word then smiling approvingly. "I like it. But only for the logo."

El clapped her hands together. "Deal!"

Completing the rest of that section of the Web site proved to be even more difficult than he'd expected. Eleanor always had a better idea on the way things should be done and let him know it. Her lack of knowledge about site building and designing drove Bob crazy as he tried his best to give in to her demands and still produce a quality product.

"It won't work that way, El!" he told her late one afternoon after a particularly trying day. "You want the impossible!"

Her chin jutted out as her hands went to her hips. "You can do it, Bob. I know you can. You're just being obstinate."

He leaped from his chair, nearly knocking it over. "Then you sit down there and show me how, Miss Know-it-all."

Eleanor glared at him, her chin still set defiantly. "I'm paying you to design the Web site and get it running. You're supposed to be doing it the way I say you should!"

Pacing about the room in exasperation, he raked his fingers through his hair. "I warned you I wasn't a pro at this. What you are asking is impossible. Why can't you see that?"

"I have faith in you, Bobby."

Though he tried to be mad at her, suddenly she was the eight-year-old girl again. Vulnerable and trusting, sure he could move mountains. "Okay, you win. I'll call a friend of mine who works for a top PC manufacturer. If there is a way to do what you ask, he'll know how to set it up." He reached out and took both her hands in his, giving them a gentle squeeze. "But you have to get out of my hair. I can't work with you leaning over my shoulder every second. I need breathing room. I can't think with you so close beside me. Don't you have other things to do? Like run your business?"

She took on a coy smile. "Do I distract you that much?"

He gave his head an embarrassed nod. "You know you do. You always have. Now go!"

Eleanor leaned toward him and kissed his cheek. "If you insist, but I'll be back. You can't get rid of me that easily. Remember, this is a joint effort."

He grinned. "Yeah, you own the joint, and I'm giving the effort. Now scoot before I—"

A well-shaped brow rose. "Before you what?"

"Before I call it a day and go home early. I barely see my kids anymore."

Eleanor backed away with a hearty laugh. "That's some threat! Is that the best you can do?"

He chuckled. "Oh, you're challenging me?"

She hurried toward the door and grabbed hold of the knob. "No! No challenge. You'd leave early just to show me who is boss. I'm going. Keep working. We need to get that Web site online by the first of October."

Smiling victoriously, Bob gave her a salute. "Okay, boss lady. Go bother someone else."

Once she had closed the door securely, Bob lifted his face heavenward. *Lord, let my light shine before El, and help me to get this Web site done. I miss my kids, and I think they miss me. I'm in way over my head. Only You can keep me afloat.*

❧

Eleanor leaned against the closed door. There was not a shadow of a doubt in her mind that Bob Rachette had her best interest at heart.

"He's one of the good guys, isn't he?" Ruthie asked as she approached Eleanor with a letter that needed her signature. "You're lucky to have him."

"Yes, Bob is one of the finest men I know." Straightening and taking on her usual business stance, Eleanor nodded, reached for the letter, and signed it. "Now get this letter in the mail. I want it to go out today."

"The mail has already been picked up."

Eleanor gave the woman an impatient glare. "Then take it to the post office on your way home!"

With only a grunt Ruthie accepted the letter.

Eleanor waited until Ruthie had disappeared down the hall, then turned back to Bob's office door, her fingers running over the nameplate that said Robert Rachette, Chief Accountant. "You are one of the good guys," she said in a mere whisper. "But like the old cliché says, 'Good guys usually finish last.' Too bad you had to burden yourself with a family at such an early age. You could have made it to the top. You're capable of much better things. Why couldn't you ever see that?"

"Maybe he is at the top! Right where I want him."

Eleanor turned quickly, surprised to find she was the only one in the outer office. Everyone else had left for the day. Who had said that? Had she imagined it? She quickly surveyed the area once more, but no one was around. "I must be tired," she said aloud. "My mind is playing tricks on me."

For the next few weeks, most of Eleanor's concentration was spent on the newspaper and television ads she had purchased to tout the new Web site, leaving Bob to work on it alone and uninterrupted. Though she popped into his office a number of times a day, usually with a tip or two on how she thought the Web site could be improved, she pretty much left any final decisions to him. He always said he was proud of the work he was doing. It was the most challenging, creative thing he had ever done. Though he clearly missed the time he normally spent with his children, he told her he was thankful for the extra pay. Even though Eleanor had told him there would be no raise, the approval for a twenty percent increase in his salary had come across his desk the day after he'd agreed to do the Web site for her.

ᴥ

"The old girl isn't as thoughtless as she wants folks to believe," he told Kari, his eldest daughter, one night as he sat at the table waiting for her to heat up his supper. "I just wish she'd had a chance to meet you and the other children."

Kari made a face as she opened the microwave and pulled out his plate. "Why? I thought you said she didn't like kids."

He picked up the saltshaker and shook it gently over his baked potato. "That's what she says, but El says a lot of things she doesn't mean."

"Then why does she say them?"

Bob glanced up at his teenage daughter's lovely face. "Good question. If I had to hazard a guess, I'd say having children means commitment, and El isn't about to let anyone tie her down."

"Doesn't she get lonely now that Mr. Scrooge has passed away?"

Bob forked a meatball and twirled it in the air. "I don't know. Eleanor likes herself. I'm not sure she needs anyone else in her life."

Kari appeared thoughtful. "That's pitiful."

He bit into the tasty meatball and chewed it slowly, savoring each bite. "You're right. It is pitiful. That's why we need to pray for her."

An adorable nine-year-old entered the kitchen, cradling a library book in her arms. "Daddy? I didn't know you were home."

Bob reached out his arms, and she ran to him. "I thought you were asleep."

Ginny climbed onto his lap and kissed his cheek. "I was waiting for you. I miss you."

Bob's gaze locked on the red mark on her otherwise unblemished little cheek. She was small for her age and the delight of his life. Though he loved his children equally, that port-wine stain made Ginny a little more special than the others. It was as if he owed her, as if he were personally responsible for her bearing that awful birthmark. How could he let another day go by without finding a way to relieve her of the agony of ridicule she faced every day? "I miss you, too, sweetie. I should have Mrs. Scrooge's Web site finished in a few weeks, and then Daddy will have more time with his little girl. Just try to be patient, okay?"

"I've been thinking, Dad," Kari said, placing a slice of the carrot cake she'd baked that day on a plate. "I'm sixteen now. The man at the corner bakery asked me if I'd be interested in working a few hours each morning before school. He needs someone to help him box up the delivery orders."

Bob placed his fork on his plate. "Before school?"

She nodded. "From four to eight each morning. That would give me plenty of time to get to school by eight thirty. He said he'd pay me a dollar more than minimum wage because he knew I'd be a good worker."

Bob gave his head a violent shake. "Twenty hours a week? Before school? Absolutely not! You need to concentrate on making the best grades you can if you want to go to college."

"Please, Dad, I want to help pay for taking that birthmark off Ginny's face."

Bob's heart was touched, and he found it hard to hold back tears. "That's such a sweet gesture, honey, and I appreciate what you're offering to do, but what you could make at the bakery in a year wouldn't begin to pay for even one of Ginny's treatments."

Blinking back her own tears, Kari stroked her little sister's hair. "We have to do something, Dad. You don't know what she goes through. People are so cruel. It's not right that she has to face their awful stares."

Bob slipped his free arm about her waist and pulled her to him. "I know, honey. I know. Somehow, we'll work this out." Though he hadn't mentioned it to his children, he was hoping Eleanor would be so pleased with his work on her Web site she would reward him with a big bonus when it was done.

"Maybe Mrs. Scrooge would help with—"

He huffed. "Mrs. Scrooge would be the last one to help. She's a self-made woman who doesn't believe in charity or benevolent acts of any kind."

"But why? She has more money than she'll ever be able to spend. You'd think a woman that wealthy would be so thankful she'd want to help other people."

Bob cradled Kari's cheek with his palm. "You'd think so, but it doesn't always work out that way. Some people value their worth by the money they have. I'm afraid Mrs. Scrooge is one of those people."

"She needs God in her life." Kari's face showed concern. "I feel sorry for her. She must be very lonely without a family."

"I think she is lonely. I know many nights she works late then goes home and eats a frozen dinner she's heated up in the microwave as she watches TV. What good is that big mansion she lives in without anyone to share it with her?"

"Maybe we should invite her to dinner again."

Bob let out a sigh. "She won't come. Now," he said, rising and pasting on a smile, "it's time for you children to get to bed." He kissed each one tenderly. "I'm the rich one. I have you."

five

On September 30, Bob worked twenty-three hours straight putting the final touches on Scrooge's Web site, arriving home on Sunday morning, just in time to take his family to church. With God's help, he had met his goal. The newly renovated, much-touted Web site was online right on schedule.

He stopped at a convenience store on the way home from church to pick up copies of the state's Sunday editions of the newspapers, turning quickly to Scrooge's full-page color ads. Eleanor had spared no expense. He wondered how many readers would hurry to their computers to check out the new Web site after reading about it. He had to admit, the ad was well done and quite eye-catching. Perhaps Eleanor knew what she was doing after all.

The phone was ringing when they entered their home. Bob hurried to answer it.

"Have you seen the TV ads?" Eleanor's excited voice asked.

"Only the newspaper ads. We just got home from church and haven't had a chance to turn on the TV."

"Hundreds of people are visiting the Web site. I've been checking the visitor counter the way you taught me. You won't believe the orders we're already receiving online. I'm so glad I decided to revamp the Web site."

Are you going to give me a little credit here? I'm the one who worked night and day to get it done on time.

"This is going to be the best Christmas Scrooge's has ever had. Our sales are going to skyrocket," she went on. "People all over the country will be doing their Christmas shopping on

59

Scrooge's dot com. I'm so anxious to tell you. . . ."

Bob's fingertips rubbed his forehead. "I'm going to have to cut this short, El. I worked on your Web site all night last night, got home this morning in time to take my family to church and Sunday school, and I'm asleep on my feet. Whatever it is will—"

"You must come into the office today," she continued as if she hadn't heard him. "I've thought of several features I want to add to the Web site. We can capitalize on the—"

"No," he said firmly, his patience wearing thin enough to snap. "I have to get some sleep, El, and I want to spend time with my family. Whatever you want to add will have to wait until tomorrow."

"But I need to—"

"Good-bye, El. I'll see you in the morning." He placed the phone back in its cradle, ignoring the still-talking voice on the other end. "That woman never knows when to quit!" he told his children as they gathered around him and gave him a group hug. "After we have lunch, let me get a couple hours of z's and we'll all go for ice cream."

୬ଈ

By two in the morning, most of the residents of Newport, Rhode Island, were sound asleep, but in the Scrooge mansion the lights in one of the upper bedrooms burned brightly as Eleanor sat in front of her computer staring at the screen. *Perhaps I should have added another jewelry line to the Web site or maybe more lingerie. Both of those items are good Christmas sellers.*

She snapped her fingers as a delicious idea occurred to her. *Maybe I should start my own signature line!* Her mind whizzed with the possibilities. *People all over the world would be wearing my fashions, my perfume, and my jewelry. What would I call my line? Eleanor's? No, that isn't hip enough. Scrooge's? No! That would never do. The name would need to be short. Memorable. It should have a youthful sound. Maybe simply El! That has a classy sound.* Her face screwed up in thought. *The name is very important. I'll have to think about it. It has to be just right.*

Moving the mouse slightly, she clicked on the tab marked *Gifts* then gazed at the dozens of gift items Bob had placed on the page—each displayed with a small Christmas motif beside it. *What good ideas Bob has. And to think he's been hiding his talent from me all this time.*

As she scanned the items, another thought occurred to her. *Maybe we should have a For Men Only section with ideas for gifts they could give their wives and sweethearts. We could even offer a special gift-wrapping service with special name tags made just for them. I'll have to talk to Bob about it. I'm sure he could add it.* Finding it difficult to contain her enthusiasm, she reached for the phone and dialed Bob's number.

"Hu-lo," a sleepy voice answered on the third ring.

"Oh, Bob, I've just had the most wonderful idea. I—"

"El? Is that you? Do you know what time it is?"

She glanced at the clock in the lower right-hand corner of the computer screen. "It's after two o'clock? I had no idea."

"Can't this wait until morning?" he asked with a yawn.

She leaned back in her chair, releasing a disappointed sigh. "I suppose so, but I really wanted to—"

"El, please, have a little mercy, okay? I've worked day and night for several months to get your Web site up on time. I've barely seen the family I love more than life itself. And, despite the good job my assistant is doing, I'm way behind in my work in the accounting department. My life has been on hold. I was hoping things would get back to normal."

She sat silently. Each word he was saying was true. He had dropped everything, with very little complaint. She should be more grateful. "I–I'm sorry, Bob. Please forgive me. I hope you won't have any trouble getting back to sleep. We'll talk tomorrow. Good night."

ಜ

Bob blinked hard at the receiver in his hand as he placed it back on its cradle. "Was I dreaming or did Eleanor just apologize? That's a first!"

He rolled over onto his side and closed his eyes, hoping to fall to sleep right away, but visions of the beautiful Eleanor flooded his mind.

Eleanor. . .the day she graduated from high school, dressed in a white ruffled dress, her long, dark hair falling softly about her shoulders.

Eleanor. . .the day she left for New York City, wearing the red suit he'd always liked on her.

Eleanor. . .the day she silently crept back into Newport. Although she'd had to hang her head and eat humble pie as she confessed her New York adventure had been a fiasco, she had looked beautiful in her faded jeans and T-shirt, her hair pulled back in a ponytail and tied with a red ribbon.

Eleanor. . .the day she'd married Everett Scrooge. She'd been a vision of loveliness wearing that fancy white satin dress with a long train billowing out behind her as she walked down the aisle. He'd never forget how beautiful she looked—or how beautiful she looked now. The Eleanor he worked with every day now was a few years older but every bit as lovely. Yes, Eleanor Baker Scrooge was one of a kind. She had the sort of natural beauty and a flair for style most women envied.

Unfortunately, she knew it.

He switched on the light, then lifted Lydia's framed picture from the nightstand, held it lovingly between his hands, and stared at his deceased wife's image. *You may not have been as beautiful on the outside as El, but you had an inner beauty that outshone her. I loved you, Lydia, and I miss you terribly. I know you never believed I loved you as much as I loved El, but I did. It was a different kind of love. Sometimes I think what I felt for El was more of an infatuation than actual love. It was exciting to be around her. You never knew what was going to happen next. For some reason I felt responsible for her. I had since the day she moved into our neighborhood and I found her crying because some of the kids had made fun of her old, worn-out clothes. She was my best friend. It seemed my duty to protect her, stand up for her, and yes, even fight for her if necessary. Fortunately, I only had to do that a couple of times.* He smiled. *Even got a black eye out of one of those fights. Oh, was my dad mad. I still feel obligated to fight for her, Lydia. I guess, if I were honest, I'd admit I still have feelings for El. I probably always will.*

He carefully placed the frame back where it belonged, lingering over it before removing his hand. *How I wish you were here with us. The kids need you, dearest Lydia. I need you. We had a great marriage, didn't we, sweetheart? You and I always seemed to be on the same wavelength. I'm glad you wanted a big family. I sure did. I was never meant to live alone, Lydia. You knew that. I'll never forget the way you took my hand when you realized you were dying and told me it was your desire that I marry again. That's the kind of woman you were—always thinking of others. What a blessing it was to be your husband and to know you loved God as much as I did. I promise you, Lydia, I'll continue to raise our children the way you wanted them to be raised, and I'll do everything in my power to make sure little Ginny gets those treatments. Short of God answering my prayer and working out a miracle, I don't know how I'm ever going to afford it, but I won't stop trying. Good night, sweetheart.*

 махорка

As soon as he arrived at work the next morning, Bob tapped on Eleanor's office door. "Okay, I'm here. This had better be good. I don't take kindly to being awakened out of a sound sleep at two in the morning." Without waiting for an invitation, he strode into her office and seated himself in the chair opposite her desk then leaned back, locking his hands behind his head.

Trying to appear contrite, she peered at him over the rim of the half-glasses she wore only when working at her computer, noticing how handsome he looked in his pale blue polo shirt and tan khakis. For a man who didn't have time to work out, he had a great-looking set of shoulders and muscular arms. "I honestly didn't know it was that late."

"I don't know how you do it, El. Staying up into the wee hours of the morning, getting to your office long before anyone else comes in. You always look—perfect, no matter what time of the day it is. Where do you get your energy?"

Appreciating his compliment and delighted that he noticed, she tilted her head and gave him a shrug. "I don't know, but, thankfully, my energy never seems to run out. I used to drive Everett crazy. That man couldn't function intelligently without ten uninterrupted hours of sleep each night. Most days, he even took a mid-afternoon nap. That drove me crazy. I hate seeing anyone waste time."

"He was an old man, El! He needed that rest," Bob countered with a laugh. Then, becoming serious, he asked, "Now tell me. What was so important you had to call me at two?"

Though she tried, Eleanor couldn't contain her excitement. "I've decided to add a whole new section to the Web site! An exciting new section that I know will add an entirely new dimension to our customers' Christmas shopping."

With a teasing smile, he lifted a skeptical brow. "You've decided to add it? I wasn't aware that you knew how to add things to the Web site."

She gave him a look of exasperation. "You know what I mean."

"Uh-huh. You mean—you've had the idea and now you expect me to do the work." He stood and shoved his hands into his pockets. "Sorry, I can't. I barely got the Web site up and running by the deadline. Except for a few changes here and there, I'm through with it. What you need now is a Webmaster. Someone to maintain it and do the regular updates, add and delete products, change the looks to match the seasons, and do all the things that need to be done to keep a first-class Web site online."

Eleanor's jaw dropped. "But you can do all those things for me!"

Giving his head a vigorous shake, he backed away a few steps, lifting his flattened palms toward her. "No, not me. I'm in charge of your accounting department. I'm no Webmaster. It's time to turn your Web site over to someone else. A professional—with time to do it justice. My part in this was supposed to be a temporary thing. Remember?"

"But—you were moonlighting, building and maintaining Web sites while you were working for me before!" she reminded him rather curtly, hoping he'd change his mind. "Why can't you do it for me?"

His face turning somber, Bob moved quickly to her desk, leaned over it and planted his palms on its highly polished surface, his face just inches from hers. "El, what I designed and placed online for the other Web sites I designed for Cal Bender's clients were peanuts compared to what I did for you. They were extremely simple jobs, requiring no more than one or two weeks to create. Once I had them up and running, they hired someone or trained someone within their business to keep them up or had Cal's company on a retainer fee."

"You're already on a retainer fee here. You work for me."

He let out a long, slow sigh, frustration showing on his

handsome face. "Yes, El, I do work for you. I'm your chief accountant. Accounting is what I was trained for—what I do best."

"I don't see why you can't do both!"

He straightened and pointed to his watch. "Because, El, there aren't enough hours in the day. Each of the jobs you want me to do is a full-time job. I cannot do both."

Eleanor glared at him. How dare he refuse her? He worked for her. Wasn't an employee supposed to do what his employer asked?

He gave her a frown. "Don't look at me that way, El. You're way out of line here. I had hoped when you called last night, you were so pleased with my work you couldn't wait until morning to tell me and congratulate me on a job well done, maybe even offer to give me a bonus, but apparently I was wrong."

Eleanor felt her temper rising. No one talked to her that way. "A bonus? Why would I give you a bonus? I pay you a regular salary to do your job. Isn't that enough?"

The look he gave her made her angry.

"No, it's not enough! Especially considering all the extra hours I had to put in to get your Web site online. If you divided my salary by the number of hours I worked on this project I'd barely be making minimum wage, not to mention the mental and physical strain of trying to please you! Which, I might add, is never easy to do."

He'd never raised his voice to her before, and it made her furious. Her heart pounded, and she felt her temperature rising. How dare he? Clenching her fists at her sides, she glared at him then blurted out, "Perhaps it would be best for everyone if you did find yourself another job!"

"Maybe it would!"

"All right, then," she told him, flailing her arm toward the open door. "Get out! You're fired! I want you out of my sight! I don't need you, Bob Rachette. I don't need anyone!"

Bob opened his mouth to say something but, instead, turned on his heel and hurried toward the door.

This was not the response she had expected. Bob rarely challenged her. Eleanor felt herself shaking with anger, and she was hurt. Of all the people in the world she'd thought would never leave her or forsake her it was Bob, and he was walking away.

Call after him. Apologize, a small voice said within her, but she didn't respond.

She couldn't.

Why should she? It was he who was in the wrong. Instead, she watched as he slammed the door behind him, flinching at the sound. *He'll come back and apologize,* she told herself confidently. *He always comes back. And when he does, I can explain what I want him to add to the Web site.*

But when he hadn't returned by shortly past noon, she hurried to the outer office to ask Ruthie if he'd left for lunch.

"You expected he'd still be here?" Ruthie asked, seeming both surprised and irritated by her question. "Bob boxed up his personal belongings and left here a little after nine. Surely you didn't think he'd stick around after you fired him, did you?"

Eleanor gave an indifferent shrug. "He'll be back."

Ruthie huffed. "I wouldn't count on it. By the set of his jaw, I'd say he's had it with you and your demands."

Eleanor sucked in a quick breath. "Mark my words, he'll be back. Bob Rachette would never leave me!"

But two days went by, and Bob didn't return. Nor did he return on the third day.

"Maybe you should call and apologize," Ruthie told her, holding up a handful of call slips. "Dozens of people are phoning, complaining about the orders they're trying to place on the Web site. It seems the shopping cart keeps rejecting their credit cards. No telling how much business we've lost."

Angrily, Eleanor grabbed them from her hands and quickly scanned through the stack. "This will never do! We have to keep our customers happy." She leaned toward Ruthie's desk and pointed to the phone. "Get Bob Rachette. I want to talk to him."

Ruthie dialed the number and waited, but when no one had answered by the fifth ring, she hung up. "Not home."

"Where could he be?" Eleanor asked, more to herself than to Ruthie.

"Probably working at a new job."

Eleanor bristled. "Surely you don't mean that."

"Knowing Bob, I'll bet he's found another job by now. That man has a family to support."

Ruthie's laugh irritated Eleanor.

"He'd never leave me. He owes me."

"He owes you? Seems to me it's the other way around. That man has worked his tail off for you."

"And I paid him well to do it!"

Ruthie picked up the stack of morning mail and began to sort through it. "Not if you pay him like you pay the rest of us."

Eleanor glared at her assistant. "Ruthie—if I didn't know better, I'd think you were challenging me to fire you, too."

Ruthie lifted a brow and gave her a shrug. "So fire me. I can start drawing my Social Security in a few months. I've been thinking about retiring anyway. My daughter and her husband have been begging me to move up to Providence and baby-sit for them while she works. Maybe it's time."

Eleanor found herself speechless, almost too upset to even respond. The idea of losing her two key people was too much to comprehend. Refusing to answer Ruthie's challenge and struggling to keep the emotion out of her voice, she said, "I'll be in my office. Let me know if you hear from Bob."

☙

"Great job, Bob. Good to have you back. The client loved it. I couldn't have done it better myself."

Bob smiled at Cal Bender, his friend and boss. "The guy was easy to work with. He knew exactly what he wanted. I just followed his instructions."

"That's not the way I heard it. That man said you were a creative genius."

Bob huffed. "A genius? Far from it."

Cal pulled a chair up close to Bob's desk. "Have you heard from Mrs. Scrooge?"

Bob saved his work then leaned back in his chair. "Not a word and I don't expect I will. She's a proud woman, Cal. She'd never admit she was wrong—about anything."

"You could come to work for me—on a full-time basis. I can't pay you as much as Mrs. Scrooge is paying you, but with the increase in business we've had this year—"

"Thanks, Cal, but no thanks. I need to make more money, not less. But I would like to continue to work for you on a part-time basis. I really need the income."

"I know. I sure wish there was some way I could help you raise the necessary funds to pay for Ginny's treatments."

"It'll take a miracle. Only God can provide that much money."

"Well, He can perform miracles. We'll continue to pray for your little girl."

Bob turned his attention back to the Web site he was designing for their newest client. "Thanks, Cal. I have faith that God will provide those funds."

"Phone for you, Bob," Cal's secretary called out from the outer office. "Some woman. Said her name was Ruthie."

Bob picked up the receiver. "Hi, Ruthie. What's up?"

"Her highness has been asking about you."

"You didn't tell her where I was, did you?"

"You asked me not to."

"Good girl."

"Scrooge's Web site shopping cart is rejecting the customers' credit cards. Our queen bee is going bonkers. She's driving us all crazy. Come back and put us out of our misery, please. You're the only one who can take care of this mess."

Even though she couldn't see it, Bob shook his head. "I can't, Ruthie. I have to stand my ground. Sooner or later, Eleanor has to realize she can't control people. We're not pawns who come at her beck and call and can be thrown away when she's through with us."

Ruthie chortled. "You're right. She even threatened to fire me."

"You? Why?"

"Insubordination. Back talk. Rebellion. Mutiny. Take your pick."

This was his fight. The last thing he wanted was get Ruthie involved. "I should never have told you where I was. I had no right to put you in the middle of this thing. This is between Eleanor and me. You had nothing to do with it."

Ruthie snickered on the other end of the line. "Hey, I'm kind of enjoying this battle. The old girl has had it coming for a long time. It's about time someone she respects sets her straight and calls her bluff."

Bob considered the situation. Even though his pay had been lower than it should have been, considering his job position and its responsibilities, he'd been happy working for El. How had this whole situation gotten so out of hand? No, he refused to have El at odds with Ruthie because of him. It was time to take her out of the equation. "Do me a favor, okay?"

"Sure, Bob. I'd do anything for you. You're one of the few good guys left on this earth. What do you want me to do? Just name it."

"Tell Eleanor the truth. Tell her I'm working for Mr. Bender until I can find another job. If she asks, give her the phone number."

There was a pause on the other end then Ruthie asked, "You're sure about this? You really want the fashion princess calling you?"

"Absolutely."

"Does this mean you're coming back to work?"

He hesitated, not sure what to say. What he really wanted was for his life to return to normal. How he'd missed the sanctity and security of his little office in the accounting department. "Depends."

"Depends? On what?"

Bob rubbed at his chin, searching his heart for an answer. "To be honest, Ruthie, I don't really know."

"Why do you take it from her, Bob? Seems to me a man with your experience could find a job without so much stress, and a whole lot better salary. Knowing Eleanor Scrooge as I do, I doubt she pays you what you're worth."

"I need this job, Ruthie. True, the pay isn't that good but it isn't only the money I need. I need the benefits that go with the job. With my family, I can't afford to be without medical and dental insurance, even for a minute."

"But you'd get those benefits with another company. Surely that's not the only reason."

Bob felt his heart constrict. "I—I have this delusion that El needs me, whether she knows it or not, and I have to be there for her. The two of us have a kinship that's hard to explain. I know it sounds dumb, since she's a successful and independent businesswoman, but I feel responsible for her. I always have, and I probably always will, no matter how badly she treats me."

"I heard you two were kind of sweet on each other when you were young. How come you never married her?"

Bob paused. Why hadn't he mustered up his courage, told Eleanor how much he loved her, and pled with her to stay in Newport rather than go off to New York City? If he had, would El have listened? Would his declaration been enough to convince her to stay? Could she have ever loved him as he loved her? "Things didn't work out for us, Ruthie. El had stars in her eyes. She wanted big city lights, success, wealth, fame." He blinked hard as visions of the wiry, independent little girl he'd rescued from the frozen pond tugged at his heart. "Life with me offered her none of those. She went her way, I went mine."

"Please don't be offended," her kindly voice said into his ear, "I know you loved Lydia, but I have to ask. Bob, are you still in love with Eleanor?"

❧

Slowly lowering herself into her desk chair, Eleanor stared at the phone. What had she done to deserve this? How dare Bob leave her? Especially now when she needed him to work on the Web site? He was the one person in all the world she'd thought she could count on. Dear, sweet, patient Bob.

Absentmindedly, she tapped her gold ballpoint pen on the desktop, her agitation about to get the better of her. And why would Ruthie, the best assistant she'd ever had, turn on her after all these years? Was there no loyalty in employees anymore? No allegiance to business owners who provided people with job opportunities and a place to grow in experience? What was this world coming to?

She snatched up the phone on its first ring, sure it was Bob begging her to rehire him. But it wasn't Bob. It was the salesman for a new line of handbags she was considering adding to the Web site. "I'm sorry. I can't talk to you about this. I have other things on my mind—other things that take priority right now. Call me next week."

Perhaps she should try to reach Bob—to see if he'd found

other employment. The thought frazzled her. Maybe he had gone to work for someone else. Maybe one of her competitors! He'd certainly had enough experience at Scrooge's to make him a valuable asset to any accounting office.

Unable to put it off any longer, Eleanor dialed Bob's home number, only to get the answering machine. Assuming he didn't have caller identification, she quickly hung up, not wanting him to know she'd called.

"You wouldn't be trying Bob Rachette's number, would you?"

Embarrassed at being caught, Eleanor grabbed up her pen and the memo pad from her desk, then glared at her assistant who had come into her office undetected. "Of course not. Why would I do such a thing? The man quit. I say good riddance. I have no use for employees who no longer want to work for me."

Ruthie sauntered toward her desk, a slight satisfied smirk on her face. "That includes me?"

Eleanor gave her chin a regal lift. "If you fit in that category—then yes."

With the smirk still in place, Ruthie placed a note on her boss's desk. "Just in case you're interested, this is the number where Bob can be reached."

Instinctively, Eleanor reached for it then pulled back. "I have no intention of calling Bob. If he wants to speak with me, he knows how to reach me."

Ruthie's brows rose, as did the corners of her mouth, when she reached for the little yellow note. "Since you feel that way about it, I'll toss it in the trash. No sense cluttering up your desk with it."

Eleanor grabbed at the little paper, barely beating Ruthie to it. "Never mind. I'll take care of it."

Backing away, Ruthie muffled a giggle and headed for the door, calling back over her shoulder, "When you talk to him, tell him hello for me."

Though rankled by her assistant's sardonic words, Eleanor fought the urge to explode, kept her peace, and didn't respond. As soon as the door closed behind Ruthie, she dialed Bob's number.

six

"Aren't you about through with this foolishness?"

Bob recognized the female voice immediately. "Hello, El," he said coolly. "I'm a bit surprised to hear from you."

The pause on the other end was deafening. Finally, in her sweetest voice, Eleanor cooed, "It's not the same here without you."

"You fired me, El."

"Only because you upset me. I—I miss you. You are coming back, aren't you?"

He missed her, too. "Is that an apology?"

"I—I guess you could call it that. I think we both reacted too quickly and said things we didn't mean."

Giving his head a shake and rolling his eyes, Bob leaned back in his chair and frowned. Maybe he had made a mistake leaving his employment at Scrooge's. He knew from experience how El often spoke before thinking things through. Though she was usually able to cover her hasty actions with some fancy verbal footwork, Bob could always tell when she'd made an oral faux pas. Yet, regardless what El said or did that was out of line, she was a master at covering her tracks. Had her sudden firing of him been one of those spur-of-the-moment things? Maybe it'd been he who had reacted too quickly. He straightened in the chair, his eyes widening, not sure how to respond.

"You have to come back. I need you. You're the only one who understands me."

Bob sucked in a deep breath and let it out slowly. "Don't

try to soft-soap me, El. We both know you'll get along fine without me."

"No, I won't."

Her voice was pleading. He almost believed her.

"Please, Bob. I don't know what to do. Thanks to you and your wonderful work on Scrooge's Web site, the customers are pouring into it, ready to purchase all sorts of things, but the shopping cart is refusing to take their orders! Our phones are ringing off the hook. Our customers are furious with us, and we're missing thousands of dollars in sales. You have to come back and fix it!"

"Don't you ever listen to me? I told you that you'd have to hire a Webmaster to keep things up."

"But I don't want to hire a Webmaster. I want you! No one cares about Scrooge's like you do. And, besides, the whole Web site will have to be changed the week of Thanksgiving to reflect our Christmas theme." Her voice softening, she added, "Please, Bob. Won't you do it for me?"

He closed his eyes and rubbed at his temples. Maybe he could go back—at least for a little while before he began looking for another job—to help her through this crisis. What difference would a few weeks make? "Okay, I'll come back, but only until after the first of the year. Is that understood?"

"Oh, Bob, this makes me so happy!" Her voice was almost giddy. "Can you come today?"

He glanced at his watch. "I'll be there in a couple of hours. I have to finish up a few things here first."

"I can hardly wait to see you."

Looking up, he noticed Cal Bender standing in the doorway. "Good-bye, El," he spoke softly into the phone before placing it back in its cradle.

"You're going back to Scrooge's?" Cal asked with a teasing smile, seating himself in a chair next to Bob's desk.

"Yeah, I guess I am. El needs me."

≈

For the next couple of months, in addition to the little time he managed to spend at his desk in the accounting department, Bob worked on the Web site, adding new features, reworking old ones, getting the Christmas theme up, and putting out fires. As with most highly trafficked Web sites, there seemed to be an endless string of problems, and problems meant a halt in business and lost sales.

"With the amount of business Scrooge's Web site is doing now," he told El with exasperation one afternoon a few days before Christmas as he stood in front of her desk, "you have no choice but to hire a full-time, professional Webmaster."

"But, Bob, I'm counting on you to—"

Holding his palms up between them, he gave his head a vigorous shake. "No, El. In case you've forgotten, I am an accountant, not a Webmaster. I crunch numbers. Accounting is what I do, and I not only enjoy it, I'm good at it."

"I'm glad you're here," she told him, ignoring his refusal and rising from her desk. "I'm holding a press conference in a few minutes. Due to the Web site and the increased business it has brought from all across the country, our Christmas sales have skyrocketed and we've exceeded our wildest expectations, so I'm going to announce the big donation I'm giving to the children's hospital in Scrooge's name. Isn't that wonderful?"

All Bob could think about was what that vast amount of money could do for little Ginny, but he knew there were other children in the world who needed help, and he was glad she was making the donation to such a worthy cause.

"They're ready for you," Ruthie said, pushing open the office door. "I told them you wanted the cameras set up in front of that big Christmas display near the front door."

Eleanor grabbed his hand and tugged him toward the open door. "Come with me, Bob. I want you there when I make the big announcement."

Dozens of people, mostly Scrooge's local customers who were curious about what was going on, were already gathered around the reporters and video cameras when Eleanor and Bob reached the front of the store.

"Do I look all right?" she asked him, glancing at her reflection in one of the store's nearby full-length mirrors.

He gave her a quick once-over. "You look beautiful!" And she did. Her beauty never ceased to amaze him.

"I'm so glad you've all come." Eleanor's smile radiated warmth and grace as she moved into the brightly lit area in front of a bank of red poinsettia plants that had been positioned especially for the press conference and took her place next to a distinguished gentleman who, no doubt, represented the children's hospital. Eleanor shook the man's hand, spoke a few words with him, and then turned her smiling face toward the cameras again.

"Several years ago," she began in a clear and deliberate voice, "I launched Scrooge's Web site, and it has been moderately successful, despite the lack of time I was able to give to it. For some time it has been my desire to revamp and make Scrooge's one of the most convenient, high-quality shopping experiences on the World Wide Web, offering our customers a vast selection of quality and tastefully fashionable merchandise. October the first, that dream became a reality as Scrooge's newly renovated and expanded Web site was launched. Due to my planning, foresight, and countless hours of hard work, customers have flocked to Scrooge's dot com to do their Christmas shopping. Because of that, Scrooge's has had the most successful Christmas season ever, with our sales reaching record numbers, exceeding our wildest expectations. Because of our customers' enthusiastic response to my dream and my vision for Scrooge's, I am able to present this sizable check to the children's hospital."

Bob's brows rose. *Your hard work? What about mine?*

"Hopefully," Eleanor went on, "next year's check will be even larger, and more precious little children can be helped. Now," she said, gesturing toward an area along the wall where a highly decorated table had been set up, complete with more pots of gorgeous red poinsettia plants and greenery, a punch bowl and cups, and trays of little Christmas cookies. "I'd like all of you to join us for refreshments, and thank you for coming."

Bob watched with amazement as Eleanor circulated among the reporters, shaking hands and giving each her most radiant smile.

"Did I do all right?" she asked him when the final reporter moved out the door and onto the street in front of the store.

"You did fine, El. You always do fine, but it would have been nice if you'd given some of the rest of us a little credit. I hardly think you single-handedly caused the increase in sales. What about the phone clerks who wrote up those sales? The people who pulled the merchandise out of the stockroom shelves? The shipping department who put them together and made sure they got to the right place? And the clerks who did the gift wrapping, and the many others who helped?" He leaned toward her, his expression serious. "And what about me? Who worked day and night to get that Web site up and running properly? And who has kept it that way since you convinced me to come back?"

Eleanor bristled. "I didn't have to convince you to come back. You came of your own free will."

"Only after you begged me!"

A sad expression came over her face. "I can't believe you're talking to me this way, Bob. You, of all people. I always thought you were on my side."

He rolled his eyes. "I am on your side, El. I've always been on your side, but a guy likes to be appreciated for what he's done. At that press conference you acted like you'd done it all."

She lowered her head, avoiding his eyes. "I didn't mean it to come off that way. You're not angry with me, are you?"

Feeling like a heel, he stepped forward and awkwardly placed his hand on her shoulder. "No, I'm not angry with you. Just disappointed, that's all. Not so much for me, but for all those other people who worked so hard to make this your best season. They deserved a little thanks, too."

"I'm going to give them each a Christmas bonus. Isn't that enough?"

"Money is nice, and I'm sure they'll appreciate it but, sometimes, a verbal thank-you and a bit of praise is what they really need. I know I need it."

His words seemed to surprise her. "You don't know how much I appreciate you and what you've done?"

He shook his head. "No, in all honesty, I don't. You're not very free with your thank-yous, El."

Standing on tiptoes, she latched onto his hand and planted a kiss on his cheek. "Consider yourself thanked. You're my rock, Bob, my anchor. I don't know what I would do without you."

A strange feeling came over him, a feeling much like the one he'd had the day Eleanor said she wanted him to take her to the prom. Her words of praise almost made him feel as if he truly was an important part of her life. "I'm glad I was able to help."

Still holding on to his hand and gazing up at him, she gave him a demure smile. "That's my Bobby."

Though Bob managed to get away from Scrooge's for a few hours that afternoon to do a little Christmas shopping for his family, he couldn't get Eleanor out of his mind. The woman was brilliant, beautiful, and so talented. She had everything, yet nothing. He almost felt sorry for her. She possessed more worldly goods than she'd ever be able to use. *What good is wealth when you don't have a family?* he asked himself as he picked up a pale blue sweater he was considering buying for Ginny. *I wouldn't trade my children for all the wealth in the world.* Suddenly, he felt like a rich man.

December 24 dawned bright and clear and cold but, despite the wintry weather, last-minute shoppers filled the aisles at Scrooge's. Bob spent the morning at his desk in the accounting office—trying to catch up on the many mundane things he'd had to put aside to work on the Web site—with plans to get out of the store no later than five o'clock and spend a pleasant Christmas Eve with his children, attending the candlelight service at their church. He'd cleared his desk of everything but one folder and was holding it, ready to slip it into the file cabinet, when Eleanor came bursting into his office, her arms loaded with papers and magazines, her eyes flashing with excitement.

"Oh, Bob, I'm so glad I caught you. I have this wonderful idea and—"

Quickly inserting the folder into the proper place, he closed the file cabinet and locked it. "Sorry. Whatever it is will have to wait. I'm about to go home."

After peering at the diamond watch on her dainty wrist—an expensive present Bob knew had been a gift from her late husband—she frowned up at him. "It's not even five o'clock! You can't leave yet."

Using both hands, he grasped her by the shoulders and leaned his face toward hers. "El! It's Christmas Eve!"

➤

So?"

"You may not have anyone to go home to, but I do. In case

you haven't noticed, the store is closed and your employees have all gone home, where I should be going." Reaching toward his desk, he picked up a gift-wrapped package and handed it to her. "But first I have something for you."

She took the crudely wrapped package and scanned it carefully. "What's this?"

A broad smile erupted across his face. "It's your Christmas present, from me and my children. They made the wrapping paper," he said proudly.

Eleanor gazed at the simple paintings on the white tissue paper—paintings of candy canes, poinsettias, and Christmas trees. "You didn't tell me they were so artistic."

"Open it."

Slowly, she pulled off the red ribbon, then the paper. "You got me a—a Bible?"

"Yes, a red leather one," he said, proudly pointing to the description on the box. "I know you like red, and I wasn't sure if you still had the Bible my parents gave you for Christmas when we were kids."

"I think I left it in New York," she confessed, a bit stunned by his gift. "I don't read the Bible anymore."

"Well, I hope you'll read this one." He moved quickly around her, gave her a friendly smile, and headed for the door. "I'll see you bright and early on December 26. Merry Christmas, El."

She rushed past him and spread her arms open wide, blocking his exit. "You can't leave yet. I haven't told you my idea."

Bob moved back into the room and settled himself in a chair. "Okay, I'm listening, but you'd better make it fast. You've got five minutes."

Eleanor beamed, barely able to contain her enthusiasm. "Do you realize Valentine's Day is just seven weeks away?"

Bob gave her a puzzled stare. "That's what you wanted to tell me?"

"I've been thinking. We need to do a Valentine's Day promotion. You know, with red hearts, lace, and cherubs, and—"

He tried to stand, but she placed her hands on his chest and pushed him back into the chair.

"El! Who cares? We don't even have Christmas and New Year's over with yet!"

"True, but with the kind of promotion I have in mind, we'll need to have it placed on the Web site at least one month early. That means we only have three weeks to get it posted. We need to get busy on it now."

"Now? You mean right now? This minute?" He tried to stand again, but she prevented it.

"Of course, I mean now. But I guess you have plans. Didn't you say something about attending a candlelight service tonight?"

"Yes, I did, El. It's something we do as a family every year."

"Well, then. We can start tomorrow!" she explained, her enthusiasm for her idea still bubbling over. "I'll meet you here about eight, and we can get on it. I've already got a head start. I've gone through dozens of old January and February magazines and clipped out pictures, and I've—"

Pushing her hands aside, Bob rose. "El, no! I'm sorry, but Christmas is a very special time for our family. It's the celebration of our Lord's birth. I'll be spending Christmas Day with my children, not working at Scrooge's on a Valentine promotion."

Used to having things her way, she winced at his words. Things were not going the way she'd planned them, and she didn't like it one bit. "But I've already reserved space in a number of newspapers, and I want to do another television campaign. If we get started on it now and do it right, it could double our—"

Bob stared at her in obvious amazement. "Look, El, I'd do

most anything for you, but leaving my family on the most important day of the year to work on a Valentine project is not one of them." He glanced at the big clock on the wall. "If my family is going to have a little supper and make it to the candlelight service on time, I've got to get out of here." He paused, giving her hand a squeeze. "You could go with us."

Laughing aloud at such a ridiculous idea, she gave her head a hearty shake. "No thanks. I can't. I have—plans. Are you sure we can't get together tomorrow? Maybe in the afternoon?"

As if trying to keep his own frustration at bay, Bob sucked in a deep breath then took her hands and enfolded them in his. "Sorry, El, but my answer is still no. I promise I'll be in bright and early the day after Christmas, and we can get started then, but I will not work on Christmas Eve or Christmas Day."

Convinced she was losing the battle and was well on the way toward irritating him to the point of quitting if she kept pushing, she reluctantly backed off.

He smiled at her in a kindly way. "If you loved the Lord like you did when you were a kid and hadn't turned your back on Him, you'd understand why celebrating the birth of Christ is so important to us. Why don't you take a few minutes during these special days and turn to the second chapter of Luke in that Bible we gave you and read the Christmas story?"

"I already know the Christmas story," she countered with a scowl.

"You may know the Christmas story, but I'm not sure you know the Christ of Christmas. Wouldn't you like to reacquaint yourself with Him? His arms are open wide and He's always ready to listen, El. I know He'd like to hear from you."

"I've made it on my own so far and have done a pretty good job of it," she told him with an indignant tilt of her chin. "I don't need Him, Bob. What did God ever do for me? I remember begging Him to help me get a good job when I moved to New

York. Did He do it? No!"

"Perhaps it wasn't His will that you stay in New York."

"Okay then. Where was He when my dad beat my mom? When he beat me and my sister?"

Bob swallowed hard. "How can I, a mere mortal, begin to explain why God does what He does? I don't know, El. All I know is He could have intervened if He'd seen fit to do so. We don't know why God does what He does. We have to take Him and His will on faith. I don't know why my precious daughter was born with a port-wine stain on her cheek. Or why He took Lydia from our family at such an early age. All I know is that He is God and He loves us. And, if we confess our sins, ask His forgiveness, and accept Christ as our Savior, we'll spend eternity in heaven with Him."

"God has certainly asked us to accept a lot on faith," she murmured, thoughtfully mulling over Bob's words.

"Yes, He has. We either accept God's Word as He's given it to us, or reject it. It's our decision. There's no other way and no shortcuts." He bent and placed a kiss on her forehead. "Merry Christmas, El."

"The same to you, Bob." She watched as he moved through the door, closing it behind him, and once again, she was alone. All alone.

Still disappointed that Bob hadn't shared her enthusiasm about the Valentine campaign, Eleanor halfheartedly moved through the empty store. Determined not to let his refusal to work over the holiday get her down, she wandered through each department, flipping on lights and making notes of items she wanted to feature on the Valentine's Day Web page. Before she knew it, it was seven o'clock. She not only hadn't had supper, she'd been so busy all day she hadn't taken time for lunch either.

After exchanging a brief holiday greeting with the night watchman, she locked up her office and headed for her expensive new sports car in the store's parking lot.

With the exception of the night watchman's car, hers was the only one left on the icy lot. After placing her designer attaché case on the seat, methodically she slid beneath the steering wheel, closed the door, and fastened her seat belt, her mind still filled with ideas for her promotion. Almost by rote, she turned the key in the ignition and moved out onto the deserted street, barely bothering to look right or left as she left the lot.

Too late, she saw it.

A huge SUV—speeding toward her, aimed directly at her door.

seven

"Lady! Lady! Are you all right?"

Eleanor could hear a man's voice but, try as she may, she couldn't answer or even turn her head.

"That crazy woman wasn't even looking! She pulled out of Scrooge's parking lot right in front of me," a woman screamed out frantically, pointing her finger toward Eleanor. "I tried to stop, but I couldn't! There wasn't time."

"Better call an ambulance quick," another voice said excitedly. "She's losing a lot of blood!"

Are they talking about me? Eleanor struggled to keep her eyes open, but they wouldn't cooperate. *My head. Oh, it hurts.*

"Hold on, lady. The ambulance is on its way."

I—I can't hold on. Sleepy. I'm so—sleepy.

❧

Eleanor. El–ean–or."

Eleanor slowly opened her eyes and stared up into the face of the most beautiful woman she'd ever seen. Her complexion boasted the smooth peaches and cream texture all women longed to achieve, her blond tresses resembled spun gold, and her eyes were as blue as the perfect sapphire in the ring Everett Scrooge had given Eleanor on their first wedding anniversary. "Who are you?"

"My name is Faith. I'm the reminder of your childhood and Christmases past."

Eleanor backed away as the woman reached out her hand. "I—I don't know you. Why are you here? Why am I here?" For the first time since opening her eyes, she glanced around at her surroundings. In the semidarkness, nothing looked familiar. "What is this place?"

"Let's just call it the Place of Memories."

"Place of Memories? That title sounds like the name of a funeral home. But I don't understand. Why are you dressed like that—in that flowing white gown? You look—like an angel. Is this some kind of joke? Are you dressed for a holiday performance of some sort?"

The woman gave her a gentle smile. "Dressed for a holiday performance? No, this is my normal attire."

Eleanor let out a gasp, her eyes widening as her hand moved to cup her mouth. "You are an angel! Is that why I'm here? I'm—dead?"

"You've been in an accident. You were injured."

"But I am still alive, aren't I?"

Faith smiled and reached out her hand again. "Yes, you're very much alive. Now come with me."

Again, Eleanor backed away, more confused and frightened than ever. "If I've been in an accident, why don't I hurt? I feel fine." She eyed the woman suspiciously. "What do you mean—you're the reminder of Christmases past?"

A calming smile formed on the woman's saintly face. "You needn't worry yourself about such things now. Come. We must hurry. We have much to do, and the time is short."

Eleanor pulled away. "I'm sorry, but I couldn't go with you, even if I wanted to. I'm planning this big Valentine promotion for Scrooge's—that's the department store I inherited from my late husband—and I have to get ready for it. It's very important. Bob Rachette and I are meeting the day after Christmas to get started on it." Eleanor frantically searched the area around her. "Where's my purse? Is my car drivable? I must get home."

Faith extended her hand again, this time grasping Eleanor's wrist with her long, slender fingers. "Everything in its time,

Eleanor. You won't need your purse where we're going. Come with me."

As if she had no will of her own her feet began to move. "You're not going to hurt me, are you?"

"No," the lovely woman answered with a laugh that sounded like tinkling bells. She cupped Eleanor's elbow, and they began to move along the dimly lit street. "I'd never hurt you. I'm here to help you."

Eleanor tried to pull away but, although the woman's grasp on her arm was light, found it impossible. "Help me? Help me do what? You must not have done your homework, or you'd know I'm a self-made woman," she boasted, feeling quite proud of her accomplishments. "I don't need your help."

Faith gave her a kindly smile. "I'm afraid you don't have a choice. You must accept my help. It's your destiny."

Again Eleanor tried to pull away, but the woman held on fast. "This is a dream, right? Any moment I'll wake up and—"

"Call it a dream if you like."

Narrowing her eyes, Eleanor cocked her head to one side and asked, "Is this some kind of trick? Some ploy by my competitors to discredit me? Make me look like a fool? Who sent you here anyway?"

"We're almost there."

Eleanor turned her head from side to side, taking in their surroundings. Something about the place seemed familiar. Had she been here before?

"Do you remember your childhood, Eleanor?"

"My childhood? Of course I do. Why do you ask?"

Gesturing with one long sweep of her hand, Faith motioned toward the area in front of them, and the whole place became illuminated.

Eleanor's eyes rounded with surprise as she stared at the scene playing out before her. There was a small but immaculately painted house set in a yard filled with flowers, and on the front porch in an old rocking chair was a woman peeling apples. A young boy sat on the porch step playing with a scruffy-looking little dog.

Eleanor gasped and pointed toward the boy. "That's Bobby!"

"Yes, that's your friend Bobby, and look at that little girl with the sad face standing on the steps of that dilapidated old house trailer next door. Her father just whipped her with his belt."

Her eyes filling with tears, Eleanor murmured in a shaky voice, "That little girl is me. I accidentally knocked over his can of beer."

⁊⁊

"Go invite Eleanor over for supper, dear," the woman on the porch told the boy as he tossed a ball into the yard and his puppy ran after it. "Tell her I'm making apple pies from those beautiful red apples you two picked this morning!"

Bobby warily approached the trash-laden yard around the old mobile home as if he feared Eleanor's father would come bursting out the front door at any minute. "Hi, El."

Sniffing and rubbing at her eyes, little Eleanor managed a slight smile. "Hi."

"Are you hurting?"

"Uh-huh. A little bit."

Bobby frowned. "You're lying, El. I can tell. You hurt really bad." Reaching out, he touched a purple bruise on her arm. "Did he do that, too?"

She nodded. "He got really mad yesterday when I tried to keep him from being mean to my sister."

"Your mom didn't help you?"

"No, 'cause she knew he'd hit her, too. Sometimes she's almost as mean as he is." Eleanor sat down on the step and motioned Bobby to sit down beside her. "It's okay. He's gone."

"Why doesn't your mom call the police? It's not right for him to be so mean to your family."

" 'Cause she's afraid." Eleanor scowled as she rubbed at her arm. "He says if she ever lets anyone know that he beats us, he won't bring his 'ployment check home, and we won't have a place to live and food to eat."

Bobby shyly slipped his arm about her shoulders and gave her a smile. "That's not fair. Mamas and daddies are supposed to take care of their families, like my mama and daddy do."

"I wish my mama was like your mama." Eleanor's face brightened. "Did your mama like the apples we picked for her this morning?"

"Yeah, she wants you to come over to our house for supper. Do you think your mother will let you come?"

Eleanor shrugged her frail shoulders. "She doesn't care what I do. She doesn't love me like your mama loves you."

"You shouldn't say that, El. All mamas love their kids."

She gave her head a vigorous shake. "No, they don't, Bobby."

He seemed puzzled by her words. "My mama said I was a gift from God."

"Mine doesn't think I'm a gift from God. Sometimes she says she wishes I was never born."

❧

Her eyes fixed on the scene, Eleanor stared at the pair. "That's exactly what my mother said. She told me that many times. She and my dad got married because she was expecting me. I was always a burden to them. They never really loved me—not like Bobby's parents loved him. Most of the time I think they hated me."

"Is that why you're so bitter, Eleanor?" Faith prodded gently. "Is that why you never trust anyone? Why you've always looked out for yourself, with little or no concern for those around you?"

Eleanor glared at her. "Is that what you think? That I'm

self-centered? That I don't care for others?"

"Do you—care for others?"

"Of course I do!" she answered indignantly, offended by Faith's inference.

"Can you give me an example of how you care for others?"

"I—I. . ." To Eleanor's surprise, she had a hard time coming up with an answer that seemed plausible. "I just presented a sizable check to the local children's hospital."

"Because you needed a tax deduction and the press conference you called to make the announcement made you look good in the eyes of the public?"

Eleanor planted her hands on her hips, her chin jutting out. "Whether you think so or not, it was a very generous gesture. I didn't have to give them that money!"

"What other things have you done that would show you care for someone besides yourself?"

Now she was on the spot. "I sent flowers to my secretary when she had her hernia operation." Truth be told, Bob had ordered the flowers and sent them in her name.

"Did you go to the hospital to see her? Tell her how much you appreciated what she does for you?"

"No." Eleanor turned her head away, unable to bear the accusing look in Faith's eyes.

"Face it, Eleanor. You've thought of no one but yourself since you became an adult."

"That's not true! I took care of my husband until he died. God rest his soul."

"You took care of him, or he took care of you?"

"It—it was a mutual arrangement."

"Finding a nurse who could stay at your home and attend to him around the clock? Is that the way you took care of him?"

"He wanted me to be at the store. Everett was more concerned about making sure Scrooge's was operating correctly than he was about having me sit by his bedside. Besides, he was on pain medication most of the time and wouldn't have even known I was there."

"But you did spend time with him those last few months, didn't you?"

"As much as I could."

"What about Robert Rachette? He's been your lifelong friend and stood by you when others wanted nothing to do with you. Have you ever done anything for him?"

"Of course, I have."

"Oh? What?"

"I—I gave him a wonderful promotion two years ago."

"Did he deserve that promotion?"

Eleanor registered a faint smile. "Yes, he's a marvelous worker."

"Then why did you wait so long to give him that promotion?"

Eleanor felt uneasy with the way the conversation was going. "It was a bottom line thing. Just like every other department at Scrooge's, the accounting department has to stay within the projected budget. Before that time, there wasn't room in the budget to give Bob that promotion and the pay raise that went with it."

"Are you saying you couldn't have cut some of the fluff from Scrooge's budget to give a hardworking, valuable employee the position and raise he deserved?"

"It's obvious you know nothing about business," Eleanor told the woman in a tone that let her know she was upset by her words. "Every successful business has to operate within its budget."

Faith leaned toward her, her pale blue eyes almost reproachful. "As I recall, when you fired your former head accountant his salary was considerably more than what you are paying Robert right now. Why didn't you start Robert out at what that man was making? Surely the former head accountant's salary was budgeted."

Feeling as though she was getting the third degree and backed into a corner, Eleanor felt a flush rise to her cheeks. "I'm not sure any of this is your business, and how do you know what I pay my employees?"

"I know everything about you, Eleanor Scrooge." With that, Faith turned back to the scene they'd been watching.

❧

"I'm glad you're attending Sunday school and church with us now, Eleanor." Mrs. Rachette reached out and pushed a dark, curly wisp from little Eleanor's forehead. "You look so pretty in that dress I made for you. You're a beautiful child, and you have such beautiful hair."

Eleanor smiled up at the lovely woman. "My mama hates my hair. She says it's too thick and too hard to brush. She says she's gonna cut it off real short."

"I'm sure she doesn't hate your hair, Eleanor," Mrs. Rachette said kindly. "Perhaps she thinks cutting it would make it easier to care for."

"El's mama is mean," Bobby inserted as Mr. Rachette turned their car into their driveway. "Almost as mean as her father."

Mr. Rachette gave his son a frown. "Bobby, you shouldn't say such things!"

"Well, she is!"

Eleanor nodded her head in agreement. "She is, Mr. Rachette. All she cares about are her soap operas and her beer. Someday, when I get old enough to get me a job, I'm going to run away from home and never come back. My parents don't love me. No one loves me!"

"You shouldn't even think such a thing, Eleanor!" Mrs. Rachette grabbed on to her and drew her close, hugging her to her bosom.

"Mr. Rachette and I love you. Bobby loves you. And I know God loves you. It says so in His Word."

Eleanor's eyes filled with tears. "If God loves me, why would He let my father beat me and my mother hate me?"

After a few minutes of silence, Mrs. Rachette bent and kissed Eleanor on the forehead. "I don't pretend to know the answer, sweet child, but one thing I do know. God loves you, and so do we. You'll always be welcome in our home."

&.

As she and Faith watched, Eleanor's heart was deeply touched by Mrs. Rachette's words and she began to weep openly. "Oh, Faith, I remember that day as if it were yesterday. Mrs. Rachette was the first person to tell me she loved me. I remember wanting to throw my arms around her neck and never let go. She and Mr. Rachette were such lovely people, always so kind and understanding, and Bobby was just like them. I thought he was the luckiest boy in the world."

"He saved your life, didn't he?"

Eleanor nodded, remembering that horrible day she ventured out onto the frozen pond despite Bobby's warning. "I could have died that day. So could Bobby."

"He came after you with no thought of his own safety."

"I know. If that ice had broken any more than what it did—"

"If it would have broken, perhaps you wouldn't be standing here now. You might not have lived to marry Everett Scrooge, and you probably wouldn't be CEO of Scrooge's and living in that fine house of yours. It seems you owe a great deal to little Robert Rachette."

Feeling an unexpected pang of guilt, Eleanor lowered her head, avoiding the woman's eyes. "I—I guess I do."

"Do you remember the best Christmas you ever had?"

Once again, Eleanor's eyes misted over. "Oh, yes. It was the year Mrs. Rachette talked my mother into letting me spend

Christmas Eve at Bobby's house. I'll never forget it."

&

Mrs. Rachette threw the door open wide. "Come on in, Eleanor. We've been waiting for you."

Young Eleanor stepped inside. The room was a fairyland of wonder, with its tall Christmas tree filled with hundreds of merrily twinkling lights casting colorful dancing shadows on the wall. "It's—it's beautiful!"

Taking her hand, Mrs. Rachette led her to the tree where the two of them stood gazing at the beautiful, illuminated star topping the uppermost branch. "I'm glad you like it. I love Christmas."

"Have a candy cane cookie. I helped make them." Bobby held out a tray laden with dozens of decorated Christmas cookies.

Each was so enticing Eleanor had a hard time making up her mind.

"You can have two if you want," Bobby said, his boyish smile widening.

Eleanor chose a red and white candy cane cookie and one shaped like a Christmas tree with green icing and sugar sparkles.

"Don't you two fill up on cookies," Mrs. Rachette warned them with a smile. "I've fixed Bobby's favorite. Meat loaf with lots of mashed potatoes and gravy."

"No one makes mashed potatoes like you, Mrs. Rachette."

"Would you like to thank the Lord for our food, Bobby?" Mr. Rachette asked once the four of them had gathered around the table and he'd lit the big red candle in the center.

Eleanor fingered the exquisite poinsettia tablecloth with matching napkins.

Bobby nodded and bowed his head. "Lord, thank You for the food my mama made for us. Thank You for my daddy who goes to work every day to make money to buy our food. Thank You for our house."

Little Eleanor opened one eye a slit and peered at the family. Each one had their head bowed and their eyes closed.

"Thank You for Jesus who was borned on Christmas and died on the cross to save us from our sins, and thank You for letting El have dinner with us. Amen."

Eleanor sat quietly, eyeing each person as the meat loaf platter and the rest of the goodies Mrs. Rachette had prepared were passed from person to person.

"Would you like whipped cream on your pumpkin pie?" Mrs. Rachette asked Eleanor, holding out a plate with a large piece of pie on it when they'd finished their meal.

"It's good," Bobby told her, his eyes sparkling as he waited his turn. "You'll like it."

Eleanor smiled expectantly at Bobby then at his mother. "Yes, thank you, I would like whipped cream on my pie."

"That was the best pie ever," she said after she'd eaten every crumb.

"It's time to read the Christmas story." Mr. Rachette pushed his chair away from the table. "Let's all gather around the Christmas tree."

After following the Rachette family into the living room, she seated herself next to Bobby on the floor near the towering tree. Mr. Rachette motioned his wife to sit down beside him then picked up the big family Bible from the table, opened it, and spread it in his lap.

Eleanor couldn't keep her eyes off the enormous Bible.

"Can anyone tell me where to find the Christmas story?"

Bobby quickly raised his hand. "I know! In the second chapter of Luke!"

Eleanor looked at Bobby in surprise.

"That's right," his father said proudly.

"Though many may deny it, the Christmas story is a true story," Mrs. Rachette added, giving Eleanor and her son a tender smile. "God did send His only Son to earth that we might have eternal life. I hope you both will listen as Bobby's father reads the Holy Scriptures."

"I'm sure they will, dear." Mr. Rachette adjusted his glasses and began to read.

Eleanor listened with rapt attention. No one in her family had ever read the Bible to her. In fact, they didn't even have a Bible at her house.

"That old innkeeper was a bad man," Bobby complained, wrinkling up his nose. "Mary and Joseph needed a place to rest. He could have let them come into his own house."

"That would have been nice of him, but perhaps he had a big family and didn't have room for them. He was nice enough to offer them space in the stable," his mother reminded him.

"At least they had shelter," Mr. Rachette added. "It was all a part of God's master plan. Our Lord was born the child of a King. The last place the cruel leaders of that day expected a king to be born was in a stable."

Bobby leaned forward, resting his elbows on his knees. "I think it's really neat the way God sent a star to lead the wise men."

With a laugh, Mr. Rachette held up a hand toward his son. "You're getting ahead of the story, Bobby."

Eleanor's eyes widened. "God really sent a star?"

Mrs. Rachette gave her arm a loving pat. "Yes, He did, honey. Listen to Mr. Rachette, and you'll hear all about it."

"You're right, sweetheart. The Christmas story is a true story. We must never forget that." After slipping his glasses back on, Bobby's father began to read. " 'And it came to pass in those days, that there went out a decree from Caesar Augustus, that all the world should be taxed. . . . And all went to be taxed, every one into his own city. And Joseph also went up from Galilee, out of the city of Nazareth, into Judaea, unto the city of David, which is called Bethlehem; (because he was of the house and lineage of David:) To be taxed with Mary his espoused wife, being great with child. And so it was, that, while they were there, the days were accomplished that she should be delivered.'"

"That meant it was time for the baby Jesus to be born," Mrs. Rachette inserted with a smile toward the children.

Mr. Rachette nodded. "That's true, and they didn't have any relatives to stay with. Do you know where they stayed while they were in Bethlehem?"

Bobby's hand shot up. "I know! They had to stay in a stable with the animals!"

"That's right, Bobby. Let's read on." His father lifted the big Bible. "'And she brought forth her firstborn son, and wrapped him in swaddling clothes, and laid him in a manger; because there was no room for them in the inn. And there were in the same country shepherds abiding in the field, keeping watch over their flock by night. And, lo, the angel of the Lord came upon them, and the glory of the Lord shone round about them: and they were sore afraid. And the angel said unto them, Fear not: for, behold, I bring you good tidings of great joy, which shall be to all people. For unto you is born this day in the city of David a Saviour, which is Christ the Lord. And this shall be a sign unto you; ye shall find the babe wrapped in swaddling clothes, lying in a manger.'"

Bobby frowned. "I've never seen an angel. Are angels real, Dad?"

"Oh, yes, Bobby, angels are very real."

"Then why can't we see them?"

"Because that's the way God wants it." Mrs. Rachette opened her arms wide, gesturing around the room. "Our guardian angels are all around us, to protect us and keep us safe."

"'And suddenly,'" Bobby's father said, reading once again,

" 'there was with the angel a multitude of the heavenly host praising God, and saying, Glory to God in the highest, and on earth peace, good will toward men. And it came to pass, as the angels were gone away from them into heaven, the shepherds said one to another, Let us now go even unto Bethlehem, and see this thing which is come to pass, which the Lord hath made known unto us. And they came with haste, and found Mary, and Joseph, and the babe lying in a manger.' "

"What about the star, Dad?"

"Oh, that's a wonderful part of the story. It's recorded in the second chapter of Matthew." Turning the pages quickly, Mr. Rachette began to read. " 'Now when Jesus was born in Bethlehem of Judaea in the days of Herod the king, behold, there came wise men from the east to Jerusalem, saying, Where is he that is born King of the Jews? For we have seen his star in the east, and are come to worship him.' "

"So there really was a star, Dad?"

"Absolutely, Son. It's recorded right there in the scriptures."

"That's a wonderful story. I like it," Eleanor said, taking on a nostalgic look once Mr. Rachette had closed the Bible and placed it back on the table. "But it's really sad those bad men didn't want Jesus to be their King. Why didn't God just send a bolt of lightning to strike them or a flood to kill them like He did when Abraham had to build the ark?"

Gently patting Eleanor's shoulder, Mrs. Rachette leaned toward her and whispered, "It was Noah who built the ark, dear, not Abraham."

Blushing, Eleanor lowered her head and began to fidget with the hem of her skirt.

"Don't be embarrassed, Eleanor," Mr. Rachette told her, pulling his glasses from his nose and slipping them into his pocket. "You haven't had the opportunity of going to church and Sunday school like most of us have. They don't teach those things in most public schools, though they should."

"I do wish your parents would let you go to church with us," Bobby's mother said. "There are so many wonderful stories in the Bible—stories every child should know. We need to ask them again."

"Yeah," Bobby chimed in. "Sunday school is great. They give us some neat prizes for memorizing scripture."

"But remember, Bobby," his father reminded him with a laugh, "getting prizes is not the only reason we should memorize God's Word. We need to hide it away in our hearts—that we might not sin against Him."

Eleanor frowned at Bobby's father. "I'm too young to sin."

"Everyone has sinned, Eleanor."

Eleanor frowned thoughtfully. "Even Bobby?"

His father nodded. "Even Bobby."

"I've—I've never sinned," Eleanor repeated defensively.

Mrs. Rachette reached down, took Eleanor's hand, and pulled her up onto her lap. "God said all have sinned. Have you ever sassed back at your father or mother? Fought with your sister? Lied about something? Maybe you even stole a pencil or another item that belonged to someone else?"

Eleanor sat speechless.

"The worst sin of all is rejecting God and His love." Bobby's mother gently stroked Eleanor's hair. "Look at it this way, sweetie. Remember that day when Bobby rescued you from the frozen pond?"

Eleanor shuddered and nodded.

"Bobby loved you so much he was willing to give up his own life, if necessary, to save yours. That's just a small example to show you what God did for us. He sent His only Son who died on the cross for us—in our place—to give us eternal life in heaven with Him. He didn't do it because we were good people. He did it because He loved us."

"Are you and Mr. Rachette going to heaven someday?"

The two nodded.

"Is Bobby?"

"Yes." Mr. Rachette placed a loving hand on Bobby's shoulder. "Last summer, during Vacation Bible School, Bobby realized he was a sinner and accepted God's love and sacrifice."

Eleanor gazed up into Bobby's father's eyes then broke into a smile. "Can I go to heaven with your family?"

Mrs. Rachette drew her close and hugged her tightly. "Oh, yes, sweetheart. God loves the little children as much as He loves the adults. That's why He made His eternal plan simple—so simple even a little child could understand it."

Eleanor asked, "How can I be sure I'm going there?"

"It's easy, El." Bobby stood and took hold of her hand, pulling her to her feet. "You just have to tell God you're a sinner, ask Him to forgive you, and invite Jesus to come and live in your heart."

Eleanor looked to Mrs. Rachette for guidance.

With a laugh, Mrs. Rachette reached out and tousled her son's hair. "Good job, Bobby. You said it all." Then turning to Eleanor, she invited her to close her eyes, bow her head, and asked Jesus to come into her heart.

"Now you're a Christian, too," Bobby said proudly when his mother finished praying with Eleanor. "We're both going to heaven someday!"

❧

Faith extended her hand, and with the tip of her finger she wiped away a tear from Eleanor's cheek.

"I'd nearly forgotten about making that decision," Eleanor admitted, swallowing at the lump in her throat. "Mr. and Mrs. Rachette were so kind to me. That was the best Christmas ever."

"Did you mean what you said that night? About acknowledging you were a sinner and asking God's forgiveness?"

Eleanor nodded. "I meant it at the time, but so much has happened since then. I'm not the same person I was then."

"No, you're not. You pulled away from the God who loves you, and money has become your god—money, power, and success."

Offended by Faith's blunt accusation, Eleanor backed away. "How dare you say such things about me? I'm a good person, not the ogre you make me out to be!"

"If I asked you to give me the names of three people who would vouch for your goodness, could you do it?"

Eleanor thought long and hard, but apart from Bobby, she could think of no one who would vouch for her.

"Your own silence condemns you."

Eleanor bristled. "I'm not dead yet. There's plenty of time for me to do good works."

"How do you know that?"

The question hit her right between the eyes. Perhaps she was dead!

"Think about your life, Eleanor Scrooge. Think about the things in your life that will last. What memorials will you leave behind? What legacies? Or will your life have been lived in vain?"

"Robert claims to be a Christian," Eleanor shouted, defensively. "What memorials will he leave behind? He has no money to give to the children's hospital. No money to give to his church. He can't even afford to pay for his daughter's operation to remove that horrible birthmark!"

"All of that may be true, but he has something you don't have."

She gave Faith a scathing glance. "Oh? And what is that?"

"He loves the Lord with all his heart, mind, and soul, and he's raising his family to love and honor God. God isn't interested in the things man or woman can do. He wants their unequivocal love and a personal relationship with each one. Wouldn't you like to renew the relationship you began that day in the Rachette living room? The day you had faith enough to believe God and ask Him to come into your heart and dwell there?"

Eleanor stared off in space, contemplating Faith's words carefully, then shook her head.

In the twinkling of an eye, Faith was gone, and Eleanor was standing alone in the darkness, an abyss that had no beginning and no end, still wondering if perhaps she had died in that car accident and was doomed to spend eternity apart from God.

eight

Suddenly a tiny shaft of light appeared off in the distance, one so tiny it was hard to make out. Trembling with fear and afraid of the darkness and what dangers may be lurking there, Eleanor rushed toward it, only to find a single, small light bulb burning in an empty room.

"Faith? Are you here?"

She waited for an answer but none came.

"Hello!" she called out. "Is anyone here?"

"I'm here," a soft, female voice came from the far corner.

Looking quickly in that direction Eleanor squinted her eyes, her heart pounding in her throat. "Where are you? I can't see you."

A woman, who looked to be about Eleanor's age and wearing a filmy white dress, stepped out of the darkness and moved toward her. She was the picture of grace and elegance, and every bit as pretty as Faith, but with red tresses and emerald green eyes that seemed to pierce Eleanor's very being. "Hello, Eleanor. I've been waiting for you."

Surprised by her sudden appearance, Eleanor's palm flattened on her chest. "Are—are you related to Faith? You look very much like her."

The woman smiled. "In some ways we're related."

"Surely you're not going to try to take me to the Place of Memories like Faith did. I really don't want to go there again. I want to go home. I have so much work to do. By the way, what's your name?"

"Hope. My name is Hope."

Eleanor eyed her suspiciously. "Are you an angel?"

"Why do you ask? Do you think I'm an angel?"

"I—I don't know, but there's a glow about you. And like Faith, you seem to float from place to place instead of walk like the rest of us do."

"Did you think Faith was an angel?"

"Not at first but there was something about her. A sweetness, a sincerity. I wasn't sure what she was."

Hope reached out her hand. "Come with me, Eleanor. It's time."

Eleanor shook her head. "No, I didn't want to go with Faith, and I don't want to go with you."

Again, Hope reached out her hand. "Come."

Though Eleanor tried to refuse her invitation, she couldn't. Something propelled her forward, and she found herself unable resist. "You're taking me to the Place of Memories, too, aren't you?"

"You really don't want to go?"

"It—it isn't that I don't want to go. I sort of enjoyed my trip down memory lane with Faith, but I have better things to do with my time. Surely you can understand since, like Faith, you seem to know all about me."

Hope reached out her hand a third time. "Come, Eleanor. We're not going down memory lane. I'm going to take you to a place in the here and now."

Though Eleanor struggled to keep her hand at her side, against her will it moved forward, and her fingers twined with Hope's.

"I know you don't believe it, Eleanor, but there are people who love you and are concerned about you."

Eleanor harrumphed. "Love is a silly word. No one truly loves another person. All they're interested in is what that person can do for them."

"Is that the reason Bobby saved your life when you went out onto the ice? Because of what he expected you to do for him?"

Eleanor rolled her eyes. "That's different. We were children."

"Then why do you think he risked his life to save yours?"

Eleanor bit at her lip, a habit she'd acquired when she didn't have a ready answer for a disgruntled customer. "I guess he didn't realize the danger he was in."

"Come on, Eleanor. Don't you remember how Bobby pleaded with you to come back? To get off the ice before something happened? He had plenty of time to think about the consequences of his actions. Face it. He loved you. You were important to him." Hope gave her hand a gentle squeeze. "He loved you then. He still does."

"I—I love him, too. I've only recently come to realize how much I love him."

"Look, Eleanor!"

Following Hope's lead, Eleanor turned quickly and found herself peering through the windows of someone's home. "Who lives here? And why are we peeking in their windows like voyeurs?"

"This is Bob Rachette's home."

Frowning with disdain, Eleanor glared at the small tract house. "This is where Bob lives? In this insignificant, ramshackle house? In this horrible neighborhood?"

"You've never been here before? I thought you said he was your friend."

Eleanor dipped her head shyly. "He is. My very best friend."

"Your very best friend and you've never been to his home? I find that a little strange. Surely you've invited him to your home."

"No, I haven't."

Hope took the tip of her garment and wiped at the hazy window. "But you have met his family, haven't you?"

"I saw them briefly once. At his wife's funeral."

"Would you like to meet them? They've just come back from the candlelight service at their church."

Eleanor backed away from the window. "No, not now!"

Instantly, she found herself and Hope standing in a hallway, less than ten feet from Bob and his children. "Now see what you've done. I told you No! I didn't want to meet them now." She smoothed at her hair. "This is so awkward."

Hope gave her shoulder a reassuring pat. "Don't worry. They can't see you. Bob is just about to fix a snack for his family."

Once Eleanor realized Hope was telling her the truth and Bob and his family really couldn't see her, she couldn't contain her smile as she gazed at Bob. He was standing in front of the microwave oven, an apron tied around his waist. She'd never seen him like that. He looked so—domestic.

"How'd you each like to have a cup of hot cocoa with a big marshmallow on top?" he asked his five children, smiling contentedly.

All but one, clapping their hands and dancing about the room, answered with a resounding, "Yes!"

Bob reached out and cupped the fifth child's chin, lifting her face to meet his. "How about you, my precious daughter? Would you not like a nice hot cup of cocoa?"

Eleanor gasped as she caught a glimpse of the girl's face. "That's Ginny! Bob told me about her birthmark!"

Hope gave her head a sad shake. "It's not a pretty sight, is it?"

Stepping forward for a better look, Eleanor shuddered. "No, it isn't. I—I hadn't realized it was so big and so—ugly."

"How would you like to have been born with a birthmark like that?"

The question caught Eleanor off guard. She'd never considered what life would be like for a child with a hideous red mark on her face. "I—I wouldn't have liked it one bit!"

"Can you imagine what life is like for Ginny? Not only can

children be very cruel, but adults as well. Everywhere Ginny goes, people stare at her. Some even make hurtful comments to her. The older she gets, the more sensitive she is about them. It tears her up inside, and she cries a lot. More than her father knows. She hides her crying from him since she knows he's doing everything he can to earn enough money for the treatments it will take to remove that birthmark. It's a very expensive procedure, you know."

"Yes, I do know. Bob has told me." Eleanor stared at Ginny. Other than the ugly red blotch that covered the lower portion of her right cheek, she was a beautiful child, with sandy red hair and blue eyes as pale as a Caribbean sea.

"Imagine what that man has gone through. The ache and pain in his heart each time he looks at that precious girl is indescribable. No pain is worse than the pain of seeing your child suffer and not be able to do anything about it."

Hope gestured toward Bob as he wrapped his arms around his daughter and kissed her forehead.

"She's lucky to have him. He's such a loving father. Not many men are as compassionate as Bob Rachette. Now imagine the agony he's experiencing, knowing he can't pay for the treatments."

"Surely there is some federal program that would help." Eleanor closed her eyes and turned her head away, the sight nearly making her ill. She'd never expected the feelings of compassion that were surging through her. "Isn't there some hospital somewhere that does this type of thing as part of a research program? Maybe a doctor who would do it pro bono, then write an article about it for a medical magazine? To, perhaps, gain some type of professional notoriety?"

Hope paused, eyeing her from head to toe before responding to her question. Finally, she asked, "Or perhaps—somewhere—there is someone who is wealthy and could well afford to pay for it as a kind gesture."

Eleanor gave an agreeing nod. "Exactly! And if they did it right, it could become a tax write-off."

Hope remained silent, her gaze fixed on Eleanor.

Shaking her head furiously, Eleanor backed away. "Oh, no. Surely you didn't mean me!"

"You could do it, couldn't you?"

With Hope's question weighing against her heart and tear-filled eyes, Eleanor turned back to look at Bob as he cradled his daughter to his chest. "There has to be another way," she whispered nearly inaudibly. "There has to be."

❧

Bob led Ginny to a nearby chair, seated himself, and then pulled her onto his lap. "I'm sorry, honey. I know you're miserable. I would be more than willing to bear your pain and embarrassment if I could. Just remember I love you, and I'm doing all I can. We just need to keep praying about this. God loves us. We have to trust He'll provide a way."

Ginny reached up and patted her father's cheek. "It's okay, Daddy. Sometimes I get a little sad. Please forgive me. I'd love to have a cup of hot cocoa."

"Why doesn't that mean lady you work for help us?" eight-year-old Bob Jr. asked, his mouth outlined with a ring of marshmallow. "I'll bet she's got lots of money."

Bob gave him a frown. "Don't talk disrespectfully about Mrs. Scrooge, Son. She's a lovely lady. It's just that her—priorities—are different than ours. She's never had a family, so she doesn't understand."

"Why doesn't she have little kids, Daddy?" five-year-old Megan asked from her place at the table, her little hands cupped about her mug of cocoa. "Doesn't she like them?"

Bob smiled at his daughter. "I'm sure she'd like little children, if she ever got to know them. You have to realize

Mrs. Scrooge has never been around little people. She's never been a mommy, so she has no idea how wonderful being a mommy is. I'm sure if she had a baby, she'd love it like your mama loved you."

"But she's stingy, right, Dad?" Bob Jr. asked, refilling his mug with more hot cocoa.

Bob paused, as if not sure how he should answer. "I wouldn't exactly say she's stingy. I'd rather say she's careful with her money, which isn't a bad thing."

"Does she put money in the offering plate at church?" Megan asked.

Bob screwed up his face. "I wish I could say she did, and that she loved our Lord as much as we do, but I doubt Mrs. Scrooge has been to church in a long time."

"Why?"

Turning to stare off in space, Bob seemed to flounder for an answer. "I don't know, sweetheart, but I do know Mrs. Scrooge needs our prayers."

Megan lifted her little hand in the air and gave her father a big smile. "I'll pray for her, Daddy."

Seeming relieved the conversation had taken a slight turn, Bob nodded at his daughter. "I think that would be very nice."

Bowing her head, Megan began. "Dear Jesus, help Mrs. Scrooge to like little kids. Amen."

Bob bent and wrapped his arm about the child. "Thank you, Megan. I'm sure God will answer, and until He does, we'll keep praying for her."

Staring thoughtfully at his father, Bob Jr. lifted a brow. "Do you actually like Mrs. Scrooge, Dad?"

Bob nodded. "Oh, yes, Son. I like her a lot. She was my first love."

Bob Jr. made a face. "Yuk! You loved her?"

Gazing off in the distance, Bob smiled the little crooked

smile Eleanor had always loved. "Yes, I've loved her ever since I was about your age. It's a little hard to explain, but at one time I saved Eleanor's life. Though I was too young to fully realize the danger the two of us were in when she nearly fell through the ice on the pond near our school, I was willing to risk my life to save hers."

The boy's eyes widened. "You really saved someone's life? Wow!"

"Yeah, I guess so. At least we both got off the ice safely. Everyone, including Eleanor, said she would have drowned if I hadn't gone out on the ice after her." Bob sat down at the table, eyeing first one child then the other. "That's an old adage that says if you save someone's life, you're responsible for them the rest of their life. I've always felt responsible for Eleanor. I guess I always will."

"But," Bob Jr. said, obviously intrigued by his father's story, "you said you loved her."

Bob paused a moment before answering. "I do love her. She's always been special to me."

"Do you love her more than our mama?" Megan asked, handing baby Janelle a marshmallow.

Bob shook his head. "Not more than your mama, honey. I loved your mama in a different way, and because of that love, God gave us five wonderful children."

"If Mrs. Scrooge wanted to be your wife, would you marry her?" Ginny asked, chiming in on the conversation for the first time.

Bob straightened in the chair. "Not unless things were different."

"What kind of different?"

"Number one: Mrs. Scrooge would have to get herself right with God and become a dedicated Christian. Number two: She'd have to love you children as much as I do. Not that she could ever take your mother's place, but she'd have to love you, want to care for you, and be there for you. And number three: She'd have to love me, and right now, I'm not sure Mrs. Scrooge loves anyone."

"Would she have to give you a raise?" Bob Jr. asked, his expression one of innocence.

Bob let out a chuckle. "Yes, I guess she'd have to give me a raise, otherwise, I wouldn't be able to support her!"

⁂

Eleanor stared at Bob. He'd actually said he loved her! "Do you suppose he meant it?" she asked Hope warily.

"I'm sure if he said it, he meant it. Like a woman, a man rarely forgets his first love. Hasn't Bob told you he loved you and wanted to marry you before you rushed off to New York to become a fashion designer?"

Eleanor searched the woman's face and found no condemnation there, which surprised her. "Yes, but I thought any love he'd felt for me disappeared when he married Lydia."

Hope gave her a kind smile. "Did you ever love him, Eleanor? Truly love him?"

Not able to mask her true feelings, Eleanor nodded. "Yes, I've never loved another man like I loved Bob."

"Would you have wanted children?"

Eleanor searched her heart. "I would have said no, years ago—but now that I've experienced life without them. . . I—I think so. Yes, I'm sure of it. With a man as loving as Bob as a husband, I know I would have. My life, although satisfying in material ways, has always lacked something. All the wealth, money, and fame I've acquired haven't given me the satisfaction I'd expected they would. Maybe a husband who loved me and a family would have been the answer—the gratification I've been seeking."

"And what about God?"

Eleanor lowered her gaze and became thoughtful. What part would God have had in her life if she'd become Mrs. Bob Rachette instead of Mrs. Everett Scrooge?

"Children are a gift from God."

"That's what Bob has always said. I've often wondered what my life would have been like if I'd married Bob instead of running off to New York. Would we have had children? Maybe a child with a birthmark like Ginny's?"

Hope leaned toward Eleanor and gently kissed her cheek before whispering in her ear, "You're about to find out."

nine

Eleanor opened her eyes and looked about the room. Where was she? It was a bedroom, but it wasn't her bedroom. Her bedroom was much larger than this one—and done in red velvet with large, dark cherrywood walls and oversized Victorian furniture. *Where am I?*

She looked down at her nightwear and found, instead of her usual expensive, pure silk designer pajamas, she was clad in a simple cotton gown trimmed with eyelet. Never, since she'd married Everett Scrooge, had she worn such a garment.

The sheets on the bed were not the luxurious Egyptian cotton she was used to—probably an inexpensive cotton and poly blend. Eleanor fingered the fabric. *What's going on? Whose house is this?*

Tossing the covers back she reached for the cotton robe at the foot of the bed and was surprised when she noticed a man's robe neatly draped over a nearby chair. The unfamiliar surroundings and the circumstances in which she found herself caused her to tense up with fear. Who had brought her here? Had someone kidnapped her? Maybe drugged her? Is that why she had no memory of how she'd arrived at this place? Was she being held for ransom?

Looking around quickly for a way to escape, she hurried toward the window only to find the room was on the second floor. Now what? How would she ever get away from her captors? Trembling and being as quiet as possible, she tiptoed across the cold hardwood floor toward the door and opened it carefully, listening for any sound from the floor below.

"You up yet, hon? Coffee's ready." A male voice echoed up the stairway.

Startled at the voice, she pressed herself against the wall and remained silent. Someone was making coffee? And why, if they were holding her for ransom, hadn't they locked her in the room?

"Come on, sleepyhead," the same voice called up cheerfully. "Rise and shine. We've got a big day ahead of us, El."

He called me El! Bob Rachette is the only one who ever called me El! It sounds like him, but why would he be in this house? Could it really be him? If it is, surely he'll help me escape.

"Yeah, Mom, hurry up. The skating rink opens in an hour."

The voice sounded like that of a young girl. Eleanor shook her head to clear it. A strange house? Bob calling her name as if nothing were awry? A young girl calling for her mother? This was all too bizarre.

"So what do you think?"

Her heart dipping into her shoes, Eleanor whirled around and found an amazingly beautiful woman standing on the landing at the head of the narrow stairway. Her flowing hair, which reached her waist, was as black and shiny as a raven's feathers. Her deep brown eyes sparkled as she spoke, and her iridescent gown filmed her slender shoulders and fell in soft folds at her feet. In many ways, she resembled Faith and Hope.

"Hello, Eleanor," the woman said in a voice as mellow as a tinkling silver bell.

"You have to be related to Faith and Hope," Eleanor told her, moving to stand before her, feeling much relieved that she probably hadn't been kidnapped after all.

"My name is Charity. Do you know what the word *charity* means?"

"I think it means love."

Charity walked slowly toward her. "Yes, it means love. Have

you ever experienced true love, Eleanor?"

A bit miffed by such a personal question coming from a stranger, Eleanor locked her arms across her chest and gave her head a slight flip before answering. "Of course I have. I married Everett Scrooge, didn't I?"

"I didn't ask you if you'd ever been married; I asked if you've ever experienced true love."

Not sure how honest she wanted to be with this person—who was perhaps only a figment of her imagination—Eleanor chose her words carefully. "I assume you're talking about the kind of love we see in movies or read about in romance novels. Though I respected Everett and enjoyed the lifestyle and companionship I had with him as his wife, the kind of love I felt for him was not that kind of love."

"So are you saying you've never experienced true love?"

For some reason, Eleanor felt compelled to be honest with this person—that she could trust her to keep her confidence. "I was truly in love—once—when I was very young," she said in an almost whisper, her gaze trained upon the huge diamond she still wore on her left hand though she'd been a widow for some time now.

"Oh? What happened? Why didn't you marry the young man?"

Eleanor frowned. "Don't play games with me, Charity. If you're like Faith and Hope, you know everything there is to know about me. You already know the answer."

Charity's deep brown eyes focused on Eleanor, making her extremely uncomfortable. "Yes, you're right. I do know the answer. That young man loved you deeply and would have done everything in his power to care for you and make you happy."

"You're talking about Bob?"

"He is the only man you ever truly loved, isn't he?"

Eleanor dipped her head shyly. "Yes, he is."

"Have you ever been sorry you took off for New York, leaving him and the engagement ring he'd bought for you behind?"

Since the woman seemed to know even the things buried in the innermost recesses of her heart, for the first time in her life, Eleanor wasn't afraid to be totally honest. No façade. No pretense. Lifting misty eyes, she began to bare her soul. "I've— I've never admitted this to anyone, not even to myself—but, yes. I have been sorry. I'm only now beginning to realize that riches and fame cannot bring you true and lasting happiness. I've missed so much—the love of an adoring husband, and although I've never told this to anyone, the love of children. Can you believe it? I've never even held a baby in my arms!"

"Not even nieces or nephews?"

"No, in fact, I've had no contact with my sister since I left for New York. Several years ago I drove by where our old trailer house had been, but it was no longer there. The lot was empty. A neighbor told me my mother died a few months after my father walked out on her, and she had no idea where my sister had gone. I never tried to find her." A pang of regret nipped at her heart. "Oh, Charity, was I so blinded by success, fame, and fortune that I turned my back on the most precious things life has to offer?"

"Only you can answer that."

"I may have nieces and nephews I've never even met." Eleanor couldn't avoid the deep sigh that escaped her lips. "So many times I've wondered what my life would have been like if I'd accepted Bob's proposal. Would we have been happy? Had a family?"

"Would you like to know what it might have been like to be Mrs. Robert Rachette?"

Eleanor gave a quick nod. "Oh, yes. I've never stopped loving Bob. He's the finest, most honest man I've ever known."

"Remember a question you asked earlier? About Ginny?"

Eleanor searched her memory. "I don't remember asking a question about Ginny."

"It wasn't a question you asked me, or Hope, or Faith. It was a question you asked yourself."

Embarrassed, Eleanor dipped her head. "You mean about her birthmark? You knew I wondered about that? I never voiced my concern to anyone."

"Yes, I knew. You wondered if you and Bob had married and had children, if one of your children would have had an awful birthmark like Ginny's."

"I–I'm not sure I could have handled it."

Charity reached out her hand. "Then come downstairs with me. Perhaps we'll find out."

When the two reached the landing at the bottom of the steps, Eleanor grabbed the railing and let out a scream. "Look! That woman in the housecoat! She's me! Bob is talking to me!"

"Yes, Eleanor, it is you. Come on; let's watch! Let's see what your life would have been like as Mrs. Robert Rachette."

ক

"There you are, sleepyhead." Bob pulled El to him and kissed her cheek. "Is baby Janelle still asleep?"

Eleanor leaned into his embrace. "She went right back to sleep after I nursed her. Like our other children, she's such a joy, a real gift from God."

Bob kissed her again. "That she is, and so are you, my beautiful wife."

Eleanor blushed. "I love you, my handsome husband, and I love your compliments. Sometimes, when I've had an especially hard day, I feel anything but beautiful, but you are always there to bolster my morale with your wonderful sweet words."

He lovingly nuzzled his chin in her hair. "I love you, too, my darling. I believe God created us to be together, and I love the family He has given us."

Suddenly, Eleanor glanced about the room with concern. "Where's Ginny?"

Bob's expression turned serious. "As usual, she's in her room. That girl spends way too much time alone. I just wish we could do something about her birthmark. She'll be in high school in a few years. I'd always hoped that by the time she was a teenager her birthmark would have been a thing of the past, but try as I may, I still can't come up with the money to pay for her treatments. I keep thinking God will provide a way."

Eleanor reached up and cupped his face between her palms. "He will, my darling. We must keep praying and never give up hope."

"I know you're right, but—"

She gently placed her hand over his mouth. "Shh. Don't even say it."

"I know. I constantly cling to the many promises He gave us in His Word, but the waiting for an answer is so hard. I've never understood how kids can be so cruel. Even some of her classmates, those who know her best, at times, treat her like a freak. No child should have to endure what she has. Ginny is such a sweet girl and would never hurt anyone. If it weren't for her friends at church, I don't know what she'd do."

A tear rolled down Eleanor's cheek. "I know. It makes me sad to see her so unhappy. I—I wish God would have given that birthmark to me instead of her. I would gladly do anything to spare her such misery."

"So would I. She's such a delicate, undemanding child. This waiting is killing me. I feel so helpless, El. I'm her father! I should be able to protect her from things that would hurt her."

"Don't put yourself down, Bob. You're a wonderful father. The very best. She's lucky to have you."

He walked to the window and stared out into their small

backyard. "I have to do something, El. Time is running out. I desperately want her to be able to live a normal life. I haven't wanted to tell you, since I knew it will upset you, but Cal Bender wants me to work even more hours for him—help him with some important computer marketing promotions."

"You'd quit Scrooge's?"

He gave his head a vigorous shake. "No, I'd never quit that job. Mr. Scrooge has been too good to me, and he's been more than fair with my salary as head of his accounting department, but it's just not enough to cover the huge expense of Ginny's treatments. Cal wants me to work more hours each weeknight and even work on Saturdays. If we save everything I make, maybe, just maybe, eventually, God will lead us to a specialist who through of the goodness of his heart would take Ginny on as a patient at a lesser fee."

"You'd be away from us more every evening and Saturdays? What would we ever do without you?"

"I don't want to be away from you and the children at all, El, but there seems to be no other way."

"I can't imagine being separated from you any more than we already are. You wouldn't even be here to lead us in our family devotions!" Eleanor circled her arms about his waist and leaned her head against his chest. "I—I wish there were some way I could help. Maybe I could take a job. I'm good at sewing. Maybe I could work in the alteration room at Scrooge's."

"I don't want you to work, El. You need to be right here at home. Kari, Ginny, and Bobby are in school all day so they wouldn't be a problem, but by the time we'd pay a baby-sitter to take care of Megan and baby Janelle there wouldn't be much left over." Bob wrapped his arms about her tightly. "God gave these five children to us, and He'll provide for them. You're the perfect mother. Our children, especially Ginny, need you here at home, and so do I."

With a sad expression, Eleanor lifted her face to his. "Then maybe I could take in a small child or two to care for during the day. With so many women holding jobs outside the home, surely someone in our neighborhood needs dependable child care."

Again Bob gave his head a hearty shake. "No, my beloved. The little bit you could bring in would help, but it wouldn't be the answer. Our God will provide. We just have to try to be patient and continue to cling to His promises."

"Though we may not have money or much of this world's good, we are wealthy, Bob Rachette. We mustn't ever forget that. We're far wealthier than your Mr. Scrooge. I feel sorry for that man. Never marrying. Never having children. He has missed so much in life."

Taking her hand in his, Bob gazed into her eyes and kissed her fingertips. "True, children are a heritage from the Lord, and so is our love. Words cannot express the love I feel for you, El."

"You're my brave hero, Bob Rachette. If you hadn't saved my life—"

"You are my life!" he told her, drawing her close again. "My love, my life, my wife, the mother of my children! What more could I ask?"

"Only that our precious daughter's birthmark be removed."

Letting her go, Bob breathed out a sigh. "Yes, that I would ask. I still can't understand why God would allow our sweet, unselfish child to be born with that awful birthmark."

"Nor can I," Eleanor confessed, "but He is God. His ways and timing are not to be questioned. I'm trusting He'll make a way, Bob. He's never failed us yet. Surely He won't now."

"My patient, adorable wife. What would I do without you and your gentle ways? Your faith in God always amazes me."

"I've learned that faith from watching you, my precious husband."

Bob's face brightened. "Always my encourager, huh?"

Eleanor grinned. "As long as I have breath."

A small hand tugged on her robe. "More cereal, Mommy."

Laughing and reaching for the empty bowl, Eleanor bent and kissed the adorable little girl seated at the table.

ะ

Charity brushed a lock of hair from Eleanor's forehead as the two of them watched the scene in the Rachette house. "Well, what do you think? Could you have been happy as Mrs. Bob Rachette?"

Weighing what she'd seen, Eleanor searched her heart. "I–I'm not really sure. Living from paycheck to paycheck isn't something I'm used to anymore. I have my credit card, and my checkbook is always in my purse. I can write a check for any purchase I desire to make without even giving it a second thought. Just last month, I went to the dealership, bought my new sports car, and paid for it, in full, with a check."

"But does that new sports car bring you satisfaction?"

"I've certainly enjoyed driving it. Next summer, I'll be able to drive around Newport with the top down. I've always wanted a convertible."

"Oh? But can that shiny new sports car keep you company on those long, lonely evenings when you rattle around in that big house all alone?"

Eleanor gave her a puzzled look. "Of course not. What a silly question. That car spends its evenings parked in my garage, where it belongs."

Charity gave her a slight smile. "My point, exactly."

"Look, Charity, I know you have a purpose in asking these foolish questions but, for once, try to see it from my point of view. I was raised in a broken-down trailer with a leaky roof. My no-good father unmercifully beat us and our mom who, by the way, was not much better than he was. There was never enough to eat in the house. My mother rarely took what few clothes we owned to the Laundromat, so we had to wear dirty, wrinkled clothes most of the time—other than when I could sneak them out and Bob's mother washed and ironed them for me. I never had lunch money, or a pair of new shoes, or a comb and brush of my own. The kids at school made fun of me because I was so poor. I know what living in poverty is like. That's the reason I wanted to go to New York. I wanted to make something of myself. Was that so wrong of me?"

"You tell me."

Eleanor sent her a look of exasperation. "I wanted to marry Bob. I really did. Refusing his proposal and that beautiful little diamond engagement ring he offered me was one of the hardest things I have ever done. I loved him, Charity. I never realized how much I loved him until I reached New York City and was sitting in my tiny, one-room apartment, searching the want ads and eating peanut butter slathered on a slice of stale bread. You wouldn't believe how much I wanted to leave New York, take the first bus back to Newport, and tell Bob I'd decided to marry him."

"Why didn't you?"

"Pride."

Though the word had been hard to say, Eleanor felt a great sense of relief just voicing it. She'd never told anyone, especially Bob, that her stupid pride was the only thing that had kept her from rushing back to him.

"Pride? Was that reason enough to give up the man you loved?"

Lowering her eyes to avoid Charity's gaze, Eleanor caught sight of the diamond and sapphire brooch pinned to her custom-tailored jacket. Though it was an expensive piece of jewelry, to her, it had become just another bauble from her jewelry box. "I thought so at the time."

"What about now? Now that you've seen a small sample of what your life might have been like as Bob's wife?"

"Since I'm being honest with you, Charity, and you seem to know these things anyway, I might as well tell you my true feelings. I long to feel Bob's arms wrapped around me, holding me so close I can feel his heartbeat. I want to be smothered by his kisses, to hear him say he loves me and wants to spend the rest of his life with me. There! Are you satisfied? Now that I've poured out my heart to you?"

Charity leaned toward her, cupping Eleanor's chin in her slim hand, lifting her gaze to meet hers. "You want all those things, but there is still something that would hold you back, isn't there?"

"Yes."

"Something more than pride?"

"Yes."

"What, Eleanor? What is holding you back?"

Eleanor bit at her lip, dreading having to reveal what she was about to admit but knowing it had to be said. "Failing."

"Failing?"

"Yes, failing at being the wife Bob deserves and failing at being a good mother to those children. Especially to Ginny. I'm—I'm just not sure I could cope with her—problem."

Charity's sweet smile blanketed her face once more. "Maybe you're being too hard on yourself. Would you like to take another glance at what your life might have been like as Mrs. Rachette?"

Eleanor brightened. "Oh, yes, could I?"

Charity spread her arms open wide, and the area was instantly flooded with light.

ten

"Bob! Guess what!" Eleanor danced into the room and threw her arms about Bob's neck. "Dr. Schopf just called! He's been in touch with an old classmate of his from medical school. His friend is now the director of the Vascular Anomalies Team at a hospital in Little Rock, Arkansas. He's offered to do Ginny's treatments for half the cost! God has answered our prayers. Our dreams for our little girl are about to come true!"

"He did?" Bob pulled her arms from about his neck, his expression suddenly becoming serious. "That's wonderful news, El, but we'll still have to come up with the other half and even half the price is going to be expensive. And what will we do about the additional costs? She'll have to take a number of flights from Newport to Little Rock, and those are going to be expensive as well. We can't send her there alone. One of us will have to go with her. Then there's the cost for a hotel. She'll probably have to spend at least one night, maybe more, each time she goes. And then there's the fee the hospital will charge. Those things will mount to thousands and thousands of dollars."

Eleanor, too, became serious. "I—I hadn't thought of that."

Bob gazed into her eyes and took on a smile as he lovingly stroked her cheek. "What's the matter with us? We're looking at all the reasons this thing can't work instead of praising God for giving us this wonderful answer to prayer! If He can work out this much, can He not work out the rest?"

Eleanor rolled her eyes. "I still can't believe our insurance won't cover at least part of it."

"They still classify the treatment of vascular birthmarks as cosmetic surgery." Bob backed away with a shrug before stuffing his hands into his pockets. "If they had to live with a child who has a port-wine stain on her sweet little face, and see what she goes through each day, they'd change their minds."

"How can they possibly call removing a port-wine stain a cosmetic treatment?"

"Beats me. Maybe because they consider it an elective treatment and not life threatening."

Eleanor moved to the sofa and sat down, motioning toward the cushion beside her.

Bob joined her, bracing his elbows on his knees and cradling his head in his hands. "I'm so sorry, El. Maybe you should've gone to New York City when we graduated high school like you'd planned, instead of accepting my proposal and marrying me. By now, you'd probably be a famous fashion designer with homes in New York, Paris, and California. I'll always be nothing but a lowly accountant, and not a very good one at that."

"Don't talk foolishness, Bob Rachette. Marrying you was the best thing I've ever done. I've not regretted it for a single moment. Fame and fortune do not necessarily bring happiness." She wrapped an arm about his shoulders and pressed her cheek against his.

"How can you say you're not a good accountant? You're a fine accountant. Mr. Scrooge has always bragged about you and your wonderful talent with figures."

"But I was never able to take the time to get my certification, El. I'd have a hard time finding a job that pays me as well as Mr. Scrooge does without that."

"Just having a piece of paper that says you're a Certified Public Accountant wouldn't make you any better at your job."

"That may be true, but you'd be surprised at the number

of businesses that wouldn't give me a second look without it. And remember, El, if it weren't for my job at Scrooge's, I'd be out in the marketplace competing with kids just out of college who have that coveted certification. Which of us do you think they'd hire?"

Eleanor carefully kneaded the muscles at the base of his neck with her fingers. "You, my darling; they'd hire you if they knew anything about you. No one would do a better job. Any business would be lucky to have you."

Bob pulled a dollar bill from his pocket and handed it to her. "Here, my number one fan and promoter. Take this until you're better paid. Having you in my corner is all I could ever ask."

Eleanor laughed then became somber once more. "Seriously, Bob. What are we going to do about Ginny? Should we go to Mr. Scrooge? He thinks so highly of you, maybe he would help."

"Everett is a decent man, but to be honest, he's a real skin-flint. I know. It's my job to account for every penny." Bob shook his head sadly. "Oh, he contributes to charities, to get some much needed tax breaks, but only to those that give him a good amount of publicity in return. He'd never help with a problem like Ginny's."

"So what's our alternative? Ginny will be ten in a few days. From all I've read on the Internet, the older she gets the more difficult it will be to remove that birthmark."

Bob stood, his shoulders sagging, and began to pace slowly about the room. "Let's face it, El. As much as we want her to have those laser treatments, we both know that birthmark will never be completely removed. The laser therapy will only take care of it temporarily."

"And she'll need more laser treatments later on. Oh, Bob, it'll never end for her, will it?"

"No, even if we can figure out a way for her to get the first few treatments, it's going to be extremely important that at the first sign of recurrence, she'll be able to have one or more treatments to keep it faded. But, from what I understand, and I'm certainly no authority on the subject, she'll have periods of time, maybe months, maybe even years, before that will occur, but it will occur, and she'll need to be treated again."

Eleanor folded her hands in her lap and leaned her head against the headrest. "But wouldn't even that be better than the way it is now?"

Bob turned toward her, a look of determination on his face. "I will find a way, El. Our little girl is going to get those treatments!"

❧

Charity shook her head. "It's very sad, isn't it? Can you imagine having a child in such need and not being able to do anything about it?"

Unable to bear the look on Bob's face, Eleanor turned away from the scene. "He should go to Everett."

"Do you think he'd help?"

She released a heavy sigh. "No. Not unless there is something in it for him. But what other source do they have?"

"Would you have helped if Bob had come to you?"

The question shot straight as an arrow to the center of Eleanor's heart. "I—I doubt it, but I had no idea what that child was going through. Or what Bob was going through."

"Did you ever ask him about his daughter?"

"No."

"Why not?"

"I—I guess I was so wrapped up in my own little world I never cared about others." She quickly wiped away a tear as it rolled down her cheek. "I was terribly selfish, wasn't I?"

"Do you want an honest answer?"

"I already know what the answer would be. I was a selfish,

self-centered, egotistical woman who cared more about the money in the cash registers at Scrooge's at the end of the day than about the man I've loved since I was a child. The man who saved my life. If I were Bob Rachette, I'd hate me!"

"Do you think he hates you?"

Eleanor lifted misty eyes. "No. Bob could never hate anyone."

"Do you think he loves you?"

"Loves me? Why should he? Even I can see that I'm totally unlovable. No one loves me."

"Maybe that love he had for you at one time has never died."

"He married Lydia."

"But only after you turned your back on him and left for New York. Surely you didn't expect him to wait a lifetime for you to return. Hadn't you made it perfectly clear to him you were going to New York to seek success and were never coming back to Newport?"

Eleanor nodded. "I—I guess I did."

"He loved Lydia, you know."

"I know. He told me she was a wonderful woman. She sounded so much like Bob—same interests, same values—and I'm sure she was the perfect mother to their children."

"Did you love him more than you loved Everett Scrooge?"

"Oh, yes." Eleanor surprised herself with her quick answer. "I loved Everett but—I'm sorry to say—as a friend. I highly respected him and his business sense, and I liked being around him. Life with him was exhilarating, exciting. His knowledge of financial affairs was boundless. I learned so much from him. That's why I've been able to be so successful at Scrooge's. I've applied the many things I learned from Everett."

"Well, as you have seen, life with Bob Rachette would not have been at all like your life with Everett Scrooge."

Eleanor looked up into Charity's eyes and found them warm and understanding. "I know. But, looking back, there was never any love life between Everett and me. Everett was already an old man when we met. We were more like business partners. He never held me in his arms, or even kissed me other than an occasional peck on the cheek. I—I missed those things."

"If you could do it all over again, knowing all you know now, would you do everything the same?"

"Do you think I made a mistake?"

"What I think doesn't matter. I'm only here to help you see for yourself."

"Even if Bob loved me, I don't think he'd want to spend the rest of his life with me."

"Oh? Why not?"

"Bob is a dedicated man of God. He'd never want to be saddled with someone who didn't share his faith. I accepted Christ as my Savior when I was a young girl, but I've never really lived for the Lord. At this point in my life, I'm not even sure I understood what it meant to accept Christ."

"Have you ever talked to Bob about it?"

"No, not really. He's tried to talk to me a number of times, but I wouldn't listen. I never wanted to acknowledge I was a sinner."

"Are you a sinner?"

Eleanor harrumphed. "According to Bob, everyone is a sinner."

"Do you believe that?"

"If God's Word says everyone is, I guess I'll have to believe it. I'm just not happy having that label dumped on me."

"Do you think anyone likes being called a sinner?"

Eleanor answered with a nervous laugh. "I doubt it. It's a pretty negative term."

"And rightly so. Sin is an ugly thing. God hates sin, but the good news is, He loves the sinner. He loves you, Eleanor Scrooge."

"I'm so ashamed of the way I've turned my back on God."

"It's never too late to get your life back on track."

"But how? What can I do to make things right with God?"

Charity placed her frail hand on Eleanor's shoulder. "Think, Eleanor. Do you remember what you did when you accepted Christ as a child?"

Eleanor frowned. "Do you mean what did I say?"

"Yes."

"I remember it as though it were yesterday. I bowed my head and asked God to forgive all the things I had done to displease Him. I told Him I believed in Him and the Lord Jesus Christ, accepted His gift of salvation, then I asked Him to come into my heart and dwell."

"And?"

"And I asked Him to help me live the way He wanted me to."

"Do you believe He saved you? That He heard your prayers?"

"I did at the time, but as I got older and my life got even harder, sometimes, I doubted He'd heard me or ever cared about me, and I turned away from Him."

"He never left you, Eleanor. You left Him. He's always loved you."

Eleanor ducked her head shyly. "Then He's the only one."

"You really don't think Bob loves you?"

"I wish he did. I've never stopped loving him."

"Have you told him you love him?"

She shook her head. "No; he'd probably laugh at me."

"Why would you think that?"

"He doesn't think I know the true meaning of love, and he's probably right. True love has eluded me most of my life. Or maybe I avoided it."

"So rather than take a chance on being hurt, you've never allowed yourself to be loved?"

Eleanor thought long and hard before answering. "I never

realized it, but now that you've asked me and I've had time to think it over, my answer would have to be yes. I've gone out of my way to avoid loving and being loved. My parents, the people who should have loved me more than anyone else in the world, hurt me more than I can tell you. I remember vowing, when I was still a very small child, that I would never let myself be put in a position where someone could hurt me."

Her eyes welling up with tears, Eleanor gazed into Charity's kind face. "I've never told anyone this before, but I want so much to be loved, Charity. I long to be madly, passionately in love with Bob, feel his kisses upon my lips, and share my life with him. But I've made such a mess of things. I'm sure in Bob's eyes I'm the most undesirable woman he knows, and God must think I'm nothing but a hopeless twit."

Charity responded with a chuckle. "If you could have one wish, Eleanor, what would it be?"

Eleanor's eyes widened. "One wish? Oh, that would be easy. If I had one wish, it would be that Bob would love me, not as a friend or as a business associate like Everett did, but really love me with an all-consuming love that takes my breath away. The kind Robert Browning had for Elizabeth Barrett. The kind he wrote about in his lovely poetry."

"And could you love him like that?"

Smiling, and without hesitation, Eleanor answered, her heart soaring at the thought. "Oh, yes, Charity. I could love him like that. I think. . ." She paused with a slight giggle. "I even think, with a little help and encouragement from Bob, I could be a good mother to his children."

"Well, you have truly changed. This Eleanor is nothing like the Eleanor whom Faith escorted to the Memory Place and Hope took to visit the Rachette home."

"I know. That was before you and Hope and Faith rolled my life out before me and I realized how stupid I've been."

"Would you like to renew your faith in God?"

"Is that possible? I've been away from Him for so long."

Faith took Eleanor's hand in hers and gave it a slight squeeze. "It's not only possible, but nothing pleases God more than to see one of His children coming back to Him."

"I so want to get things right with God. I want to love and serve Him like Bob does."

"Be careful what you say. That could mean a complete change of your lifestyle. You may not be as ready as you think you are."

Eleanor began to weep openly. "Though my life is filled with worldly things, my heart is empty and I'm so alone. I am ready to change, Charity. I just hope it's not too late."

"It's never too late to change." Charity reached out and stroked Eleanor's hair. "You've seen what your life was, you've seen what it is now, and you've seen what it might have been. Through all of this, you've come to realize the true meaning of love. God is love and He loves you. Never forget it."

"Thanks to you, Hope, and Faith, I really have learned the true meaning of love." Eleanor wrapped her arms around Charity and hugged her tight. "Thank you, Charity. Thank you for your patience and understanding—and for all you've done."

Smiling and pushing away from her grasp, Charity slowly backed away. "I'm leaving you now, Eleanor. You no longer have need of me."

Before Eleanor could blink, Charity was gone.

eleven

Voices. She could hear voices. Eleanor strained at her heavy eyelids, struggling to force them open, but they refused to cooperate.

"Looks like she's coming around," an unfamiliar voice said from somewhere nearby.

Willing her eyes to open, Eleanor peered through the tiny slits and found a man in a white lab coat peering at her. Where was she?

"It's all right," the man said in a gentle voice. "You're in the emergency room at Newport General Hospital. I'm Dr. Fryer. You've been in an accident. How do you feel?"

"Fine. Just a little surprised to be here."

"Anything hurt?" the doctor asked as he checked her pupils. "Besides the bump on your head, that is," he added when she touched the small knot and flinched.

Eleanor moved her extremities carefully, then confidently. "No. What happened to me?"

"The officer who worked your case said your car was hit broadside when you pulled out of a parking lot. You're lucky to be alive. Other than that nasty bump on your head, a few external scuffs from the air bag, and a bloody nose, you seem to be okay."

Eleanor shuddered as the dreadful scene came flooding back into her mind. "I—I remember now. What about the people in the other car? Was anyone hurt?"

He shook his head. "Just shaken up a bit. No real injuries. We checked them out and sent them on home. Nice couple."

"I'm so glad they weren't injured." Momentarily forgetting about the diamond watch on her wrist, Eleanor glanced about the room in search of a clock. "How long have I been here?"

"Not long. How many fingers am I holding up?"

"Two."

"Good." The doctor gave her arm a slight pat. "Not a very pleasant way to spend Christmas Eve. Oh, by the way, your husband is in the waiting room. Once I'm convinced you're fully conscious and there are no more apparent injuries, I'll release you and he can take you home."

Husband?

Both hers and the doctor's gaze went to the little curtain around the cubicle as it was pushed aside and Bob entered, his face filled with concern. Leaning over her, he clasped her hand in his. "Oh, El, I've been so worried about you."

Eleanor stared up into his handsome face. Dear, sweet Bob. She should have known it was he. "How did you know I was here?"

His brows rose, as if in surprise. "The officer who called me said you'd been asking for me."

"I had?"

The doctor chuckled. "At least a dozen times. You kept repeating your husband's name over and over, asking someone to call him."

"I'm not her husband," Bob said, seeming embarrassed. "She—she's my boss."

"I'm sorry. I assumed by the way she begged us to call you right away. . ." The doctor turned to Eleanor with a puzzled expression. "You're wearing a wedding ring—"

"Her husband passed away several years ago," Bob inserted quickly before she could answer.

Dr. Fryer eyed first one and then the other, as if thoroughly confused. "But you'll be the one taking her home? Right?"

"If she wants me to."

"I guess that decision is up to her." The doctor motioned toward the bandage on Eleanor's head. "With the kind of blow you sustained in the accident, you may find yourself a little light-headed at times. You shouldn't be alone for at least twenty-four hours. There is someone to take care of you at home, isn't there?"

"No. I live alone."

"Don't worry about her, Doctor. I'll see to it someone is with her," Bob volunteered, much to Eleanor's surprise.

Dr. Fryer picked up her chart from the nightstand. "In that case, I'll go fill out the necessary papers, sign her release, and the two of you can be on your way."

Once he was gone, Eleanor gazed up into Bob's worried face. "It's Christmas Eve, Bob. You can't leave your family to take care of me."

"I'm not going to leave my family, El. You're coming home with me." He lifted her hand and kissed her fingertips. "Our home is small and crowded, but nothing would make us happier than to share it with you."

"Your children won't want me around. They hate me." A tear rolled down her cheek.

Bob frowned. "Why would you say something like that, El? You've barely met my children. They're sweet kids. Of course they'll want you around."

The scene she had witnessed with Charity in the Rachette home filled her mind. "No, they won't. Bob Jr. says I'm mean, and Megan thinks I don't like little children."

Bob backed away, his face contorted with amazement. "El? Why would you make such a statement? You've never spent any time with my children."

"I—I just know it," she answered, afraid to mention the

visions, dreams, or whatever it was she had seen with Faith, Hope, and Charity.

"I'm glad you're going to have a chance to get to know my family. I know you've never liked children, but these kids of mine are really special. They—"

"I will like them, Bob," Eleanor inserted, "even love them—because they're your children. That makes them special. But I don't want to be a burden. Are you sure you want to take me home with you? Your family won't be upset at having me there?"

"All taken care of," Dr. Fryer announced, entering the cubicle with a smile. "You're free to go. Try to get a good night's rest, take it easy all day tomorrow, and by tomorrow evening at this time, other than a possible black eye and a sore nose, you should be nearly back to normal. I'll need to see you in four days to take out those stitches."

He handed Bob a small plastic bag. "Most of the pharmacies are closed for the holidays so here are a few pain pills, in case she needs them. Call me if she experiences anything unusual."

Bob shoved the bag into his pocket then eagerly shook the doctor's hand. "Thank you, Dr. Fryer, for taking such good care of El, and Merry Christmas."

The doctor nodded to each of them. "Merry Christmas to the two of you. An orderly will be here in a moment with a wheelchair."

Eleanor flinched at his words. "Wheelchair? Why? I can walk just fine."

Dr. Fry grinned. "Hospital procedure." Then, turning to Bob, he suggested, "Why don't you go ahead and bring your car around to the Emergency Room entrance. The orderly will meet you there."

Bob glanced at Eleanor. "But—"

"She'll be fine," he assured Bob. "Go on. Get your car."

With a heart overflowing with love and gratitude, Eleanor watched him go. Never in her wildest dreams did she think she would be spending Christmas with Bob and his family. Just the thought of it made her giddy.

"Sorry," he told her as they turned into the driveway of his modest home. "I know my old car is nothing like that new sports car of yours, but I hope you weren't too uncomfortable." After turning off the engine and racing around to open her door, Bob slipped an arm about her waist, assisted her from the passenger seat, and the two of them started up the sidewalk toward his house.

"Your car was just fine and quite comfortable, Bob." Eleanor shrugged. "After the accident, I doubt that car of mine is even drivable."

Bob inserted the key in the lock, pushed open the front door and, immediately, the two were surrounded by smiling faces. "El," he said proudly, leading her to stand in front of a small Christmas tree filled with lights and homemade decorations, "these are my children. Kari, Bob Jr., and Megan." Stooping, he picked up a darling little girl who was not much more than a baby. "And this is our precious little Janelle."

"She's beautiful." It was all Eleanor could do to keep from snatching the adorable child from his arms.

"And spoiled," Bob Jr. volunteered, grinning.

Frowning, Bob glanced around the room. "Where's Ginny?"

"I'm here, Daddy."

Eager to meet Ginny after hearing so much about her, Eleanor turned toward the kitchen door, muffling a gasp when the girl appeared in the doorway. Though frail, Ginny was quite lovely, with long, sandy red hair and pale blue eyes, which, to Eleanor, seemed sad. But what set her apart from any other girl her age Eleanor had ever seen was the bright pinkish red blotch on the girl's lower right cheek. It appeared even larger and darker than she had expected. The sight took her breath away.

Bob eagerly took the girl's hand and tugged her into the small, but cozy living room. "Honey, I want you to meet Mrs. Scrooge."

Forcing a smile, Eleanor fought back tears as she gazed at the young girl's face. "Hello, Ginny. It's so nice to meet you. Your father talks about you and your siblings all the time."

The corners of Ginny's mouth tipped upward, but Eleanor could tell her heart wasn't in it. "It's nice to meet you, too, Mrs. Scrooge."

"Mrs. Scrooge was involved in a car accident this evening. That's why she's wearing that bandage on her head. The doctor said she shouldn't be left alone for the next twenty-four hours. Since she has no one at home to take care of her, she's going to be staying with us," Bob told his children with an infectious smile. Then motioning toward Kari, he announced, "She'll be staying in Bob Jr.'s room. Perhaps you and Ginny would like to go change the sheets and freshen the room up a bit."

Without further instruction, the two girls disappeared up the stairway.

Bob Jr. seated himself on the corner of the sofa. "Looks like we're gonna miss the candlelight service, huh, Dad?"

Bob quickly glanced at his watch. "I'm sorry, Bobby."

Bobby shrugged. "It's okay. We can go next year."

"It's my fault," Eleanor said quickly, not wanting Bob to take the blame. "If I hadn't been so careless and had my mind on other things, perhaps I would have seen that car coming and avoided the accident. I asked the doctor to call your father, and he was kind enough to come to the hospital, then he invited me here. But if I'll be in the way—"

"Nonsense!" Bob shook his finger at her. "You could never be in the way. We're glad to have you here." He led her to a small chair in front of the fireplace and waited until she was seated. "I'm sure the children have already eaten. You sit right here while I go warm us a bowl of the soup Kari made. It's a tradition at our house to have her creamy potato soup on Christmas Eve."

"I don't want to be a bother." Eleanor started to rise, but Bob took hold of her arm and prevented it.

"No bother at all. I'm sure you're as hungry as I am. I'll be right back."

"Are you hurting, Mrs. Scrooge?" Megan asked, her little voice filled with concern. "I could ask Daddy to get you an aspirin."

"No, Megan, I'm fine. Just a bit sore, but thank you for asking." Eleanor smiled at the child. "Is that your dolly over there?"

"Uh-huh. My daddy gave her to me for my birthday a long time ago." Megan hurried to retrieve the doll from the sofa.

Eleanor reached out her hand. "May I hold it? I never had a doll when I was your age."

Megan placed the worn-out doll in Eleanor's lap then scooted into the chair beside her, her big blue eyes rounded. "You never had a dolly?"

Fingering the doll, Eleanor's thoughts went to her childhood. Her father had always said dolls were silly and too expensive, and he refused to buy them for her, although he always found the money to buy beer and cigarettes. "No, not until I was much older and could afford to buy them for myself. I have a huge collection of dolls at my house. Big, beautiful dolls in elegant dresses. Would you like to see them sometime?"

Megan's eyes lit up. "Oh, yes, could I? I love dolls. When I get big, I'm going to have a whole bedroom full of dolls."

"What about you, Bobby?" Eleanor asked, eager to engage the boy in conversation. "What sort of things do you like?

Video games? Skateboards? Bicycling?"

Bobby grinned, and she could see she'd struck a chord.

"I like all those things. I'm hoping to get a bicycle for Christmas, but I don't think my father can afford one." He shrugged. "But that's okay. I know he needs to save his money so Ginny can get her birthmark removed. That's more important than a bicycle."

His unselfish attitude surprised Eleanor. "You don't mind going without a bicycle?"

"Naw. My neighbor lets me ride his sometimes."

She turned toward little Janelle who was now sitting on the floor playing with a pile of alphabet blocks, stacking them up, clapping and laughing with glee when they all came tumbling down. "What about your little sister? What does she want for Christmas?"

Megan sat down on the floor and kissed her little sister on the cheek. "I think she wants a doll, too, and maybe a new dress."

Eleanor eyed the simple, calico frock the child was wearing. "Wouldn't you like a new dress, too? Maybe something frilly, with lace, satin ribbon, and flowers on it?"

"That would be nice." Megan scooted past Janelle and took a book from a small basket on the floor. Then, without being invited, she climbed onto Eleanor's lap, wiggling around to make herself comfortable. At first, Eleanor didn't know how to respond, but as the little girl snuggled in close, she allowed herself to wrap her arms about Megan.

Megan tilted her shining face upward. "Would you read this to me?"

Hesitantly, she took the book from Megan's hands. "I'm sure I'm not very good at reading children's stories, but I'll do my best."

"It's the story of the little lamb who wandered off and Jesus had to go find him," Megan told her simply. "It's my favorite story."

"I see." Eleanor opened the book and began to read. "Once upon a time, Fluffy, the littlest lamb in the flock, decided it was such a beautiful day he would take a walk all by himself, without any of the other lambs, though the shepherd had told them never to venture out by themselves, for fear they would get lost."

Megan sat as still as a brook on a windless day, listening intently as Eleanor continued to read, occasionally lifting her little head long enough to give Eleanor a winsome smile. "I love that story," she said when the last page had been read and the book closed.

"I loved reading it to you," Eleanor told her honestly, giving her a hug. "Maybe we can read another book tomorrow."

"Soup's hot!" Bob strode into the room and, after motioning his daughter off her lap, placed a tray on the coffee table in front of Eleanor.

Eleanor gave him a grateful smile. "It smells wonderful."

Bob seated himself on a nearby chair. "Let's pray."

Eleanor awkwardly bowed her head.

"Thank You, Lord, for bringing Eleanor safely through that accident. We know, without Your protection, she could have been seriously injured. Thank You for her willingness to come to our home and for the privilege she's given us of taking care of her these next few hours. And most of all, thank You for this food Kari so willingly prepared for us. In Your name I pray. Amen."

Eleanor gulped hard at the lump in her throat, his words touching her deeply. Privilege? He looked at taking care of her as a privilege? After placing the paper napkin on her lap, she gave him a demure smile and picked up her bowl.

The soup was good, even better than the soup at her favorite restaurant. Soon she had consumed the entire bowl's contents.

"Would you like more?" Bob asked, reaching out his hand.

"No, thank you. It was delicious, but I couldn't eat another bite."

"The room's clean, and the bed has fresh sheets," Kari announced, smiling, as she and her sister came bounding back into the room. "We put clean towels, washcloths, and a new bar of soap on the dresser. Everything is ready for you, Mrs. Scrooge."

"Thank you, girls. I hope I'm not being too much trouble."

Kari's smile broadened. "No trouble at all. We love having company. Just let us know if you need anything else."

Eleanor thanked them, but couldn't help noticing how Ginny hung back, letting her sister take charge and speak for both of them. How awful it must be for her to go through life with that horrific port-wine stain on her face. Though Eleanor had seen others with such birthmarks, she'd never personally known anyone with one. It would take very special parents to raise a child with a birthmark like that, and her heart went out to Ginny.

In some ways, she and Ginny were alike. Not that Eleanor had any idea what it was like to face life with a birthmark; she didn't. But she knew about rejection. Rejection by her parents, her classmates, even her teachers, because she was so poor and came from one of the few dysfunctional families in their school district. Words hurt. She had felt their sting many times and had wished to die. Ginny must feel like that, too. If only there were something she could do for the child.

You can, a small voice said from within her. *You have the power to help her, but only you can make the decision to do it.*

Eleanor shifted nervously in her seat. Maybe she could help Ginny.

Bob rose and clapped his hands, getting everyone's attention.

He lifted little Janelle from her place on the floor and handed her to Ginny then kissed each one after telling them how much he loved them. "Now! Say good night to Mrs. Scrooge then off to bed with all of you. Tomorrow is a busy day. We'll be celebrating Jesus' birthday."

"Good night, Mrs. Scrooge," they said in unison, each giving her a smile that told her she was indeed welcome in their home.

Feeling very special, she answered, "Good night, children."

Once the room was empty and only the two of them remained, Eleanor turned to Bob. "I need to go somewhere. Will you take me?"

He stared at her. "Now? It's nearly nine o'clock! Nothing is open on Christmas Eve. And didn't the doctor tell you to rest? I doubt he wanted you out gallivanting around this evening."

"Please, Bob, humor me. This is important to me."

His expression hardened. "No, Eleanor. It's Christmas. Surely you don't expect us to work on your Valentine project on Christmas Eve!"

Laughing, she shook her head. "No, the Valentine project is the last thing on my mind. It's something else. Something I have to do, and I need your help."

"Well. . ." He paused and stared at her for a moment before going on. "I know how stubborn you can be. If you really feel whatever this errand you want to run is important, and if you're sure you feel up to it, I guess—"

"Thank you, Bob. It is important to me."

"But, whatever it is, it isn't going to take long, I hope. I'm going to see to it you get your rest."

"It won't take long. I promise."

"Where are we going?"

"To Scrooge's. I need to do something of extreme importance."

He frowned. "But not to work on the Valentine project?"

"No." She gave him a slight smile. "Not the Valentine project or any other promotion, I promise."

さ

With the streets nearly empty, it took them hardly any time to reach Scrooge's.

"I'm sorry I had to ask you to bring me here on Christmas Eve when you probably have presents to wrap for your children."

He climbed out of the car, opened her door, and reached out his hand. "As usual, El, your wish is my command. I've never been good at refusing anything you've asked of me."

Her expression sobered as she slipped her hand into his. "I have been that demanding, haven't I, Bob? I'm so sorry."

Grinning slightly, he pulled her to her feet and cupped her elbow as they walked up to the door. "I'd prefer to call it being persistent rather than demanding."

"I mean it, Bob." She pulled a ring of keys from her purse and inserted one in the keyhole of the big glass door, giving it a turn. "I am sorry. I've only now begun to realize how rude and unreasonable I've been. Not just to you, but to everyone I know." Overcome with emotion as they moved inside she lowered her eyes, avoiding his gaze. "I've been selfish, self-centered, and egotistical, with no regard for anyone but myself. I—I don't know how any of you could stand being around me."

He closed and relocked the door before slipping a finger beneath her chin and lifting her face to his. "El? What's going on? I've never heard you talk this way."

Remembering Charity's words, Eleanor fought back tears of regret as they moved into the dimly lit store. "You wouldn't believe it if I told you. Let's just say I've recently had a long, hard look at my past, and I don't like what I've seen. If I could. . ." Pausing, she bit at her lip. "If I could change things, I would. I've missed so much of what life has to offer."

"But, El, think of what you've achieved. You've made a name for yourself in the fashion world. You own a successful business. You have more money than you could possibly ever spend. You're—"

"None of those things really matter, Bob. I can see that now. You're the one who is successful. You're a kind, gentle, wonderful, caring man. Everyone loves you, and you have a family who adores you."

Bob stared at her, evidently amazed by her behavior. "None of those things really matter? Those are the things you've wanted, El. The things you've worked for. You left me to go find them in New York!"

"I was wrong! So wrong! I should never have left you!" Gently touching his face, she gave freedom to her tears. "Do you think you could ever find it in your heart to forgive me for being such a fool?"

❧

Bob stood mesmerized, not sure how to respond to her confession. Could these words actually be coming from El's mouth? He couldn't remember the last time Eleanor Scrooge had owned up to being wrong—about anything! "Aren't you feeling well, El?"

She gave him a look of frustration. "Oh, Bob, can't you see? I feel fine, physically; it's my heart that hurts. To think what I've done to you and the others—"

"Perhaps you should see a doctor." He reached out and placed his hand on her forehead. "You do seem a bit warm."

Eleanor rolled her eyes and pushed his hand away. "Why can't you understand, Bob? I've changed! I'm tired of the old Eleanor. I want to be more like you. I—I want people to like me—not for what I can do for them but for the kind of woman I am. I have so much to make up for—to so many people I've wronged."

"I'm not sure what you mean—changed." None of this made any sense. "How could this be, El? Just a few hours ago you were snapping at your employees and begrudging the menial Christmas bonuses I'd put in their checks. You even griped at me for not wanting to work on Christmas Day."

"I know, and I apologize for my insolent behavior. I've been thinking about that Christmas bonus. I want you to quadruple the amount when you make out their next paycheck and add a note telling them it's a New Year's bonus."

"Quadruple their bonuses?" He shook his head sadly. "Now I know something's wrong. You're delirious."

"There's nothing wrong with me but an attack of guilt. I've wronged so many people, and I plan to make amends—starting with you."

"You owe me nothing, El." Bob moved to a row of switches, flipped a few, and the massive room filled with light.

Eleanor reached out and cupped his shoulders with both hands, giving him a slight shake. "No! I owe you everything. My life! Even my success. You were always there, working quietly in the background, encouraging me, standing by me when no one else wanted anything to do with me. You've always been my hero."

Embarrassed by such words of praise, Bob pulled from her grasp and gazed at the many items displayed on the counters and racks around them. "Why did we come here, El? What was so important that you needed to come to Scrooge's on Christmas Eve?"

Her eyes now sparkling, Eleanor turned and grabbed a large, flat cart from a storage room and headed for the children's wear department. "Here. You push this and follow me. I have lots of shopping to do, and you're going to help me!"

Mystified by her words and her newfound enthusiasm, he allowed her to drag him along. "You expect me to help you? I don't know anything about fashion and such."

"Sizes, Bob; I need sizes," she said, her voice fairly tinkling with excitement. "I want to give your children the best Christmas they've ever had. Fancy dresses and shoes for the girls. . . Shirts, ties, pants, and shoes for Bob Jr. . . Jeans, T-shirts, tennies, underwear, socks, toys—everything a child could want or need."

"But—"

Eleanor pressed a finger to his lips. "Don't even say it. I'm doing this because I want to. Nothing would give me more pleasure than to watch their faces as they open their presents Christmas morning." Turning back to the vast selection before them, she grinned. "Come on! Hurry; we have much to do!"

Bob watched in amazement as the woman turned into a human dynamo, rushing from counter to counter, rack to rack, stuffing clothing and other items into bags and handing them to him. After they'd stuffed five large bags, one for each child, she hustled him off toward the toy department.

"Enough, El!" he told her, shaking his head as they stood in the midst of toys, dolls, games, and other items any child would enjoy. "The clothing alone is way more than they need. My kids will be thrilled with new things to wear. You don't need to get them any toys."

Eleanor threw back her head with a joyous laugh. "Surely you wouldn't deny me the pleasure of giving them toys, would you? Aren't you the one who always told me it was more blessed to give than to receive? I've only now begun to understand what that means."

"But, El—"

He flinched as she tossed him a football.

She giggled. "Good catch! That's for Bobby. Now I want to select a bicycle for him. What kind of a bicycle do you think he'd like?"

Speechless, Bob placed the ball on the cart.

After Eleanor selected the most expensive bicycle the store carried and convinced Bob to put it onto the cart, she fairly danced as she moved from one counter to another, pulling off the type of items that would top any child's wish list and handing them to him. "I don't know when I've had so much fun!" she said, her face shining with excitement.

"You are feeling all right, aren't you? That was a pretty nasty bump you had."

She whirled around, her laughter echoing through the store. "I've never felt better! Oh, Bob, if only you could have been with me, heard what Faith, Hope, and Charity told me, you would understand and—"

Something was definitely wrong. "Faith, Hope, and Charity? What are you talking about, El?" He latched onto her hand and tried to maneuver her to a nearby chair but she shoved him away.

"I know you think I'm crazy, but I'm not! Honest! When I was in the hospital, I had a vision, a dream, or something. I'm not really sure what—but three women came to me and took me through my life. Faith took me to my past. Oh, Bob, I actually saw you save my life and keep me from drowning as you scooted across the ice and pulled me back to safety. You were so brave. You—"

"Maybe you'd better let me call your doctor."

"It did happen, Bob. Really it did. Then Hope took me to my present life and for the first time I realized how little I actually had. Oh, I had money and fame and a big fancy house but no one to share it with. No one who loved me and wanted to be with me."

Bob wanted so much to pull her into his arms and tell her he loved her and wanted to be with her forever, but he knew that wasn't possible. She could never love him like he loved her. Hadn't she proved that when she went to New York?

She began to cry. "I've never even known the joy of holding a baby to my breast."

Unable to stand it any longer, Bob reached out his arms, and she ran into them. "It's okay, El. Don't cry, please."

Pressing her face against his chest, she sobbed openly. "Then Charity came. She showed me what my life could have been if I'd made the right choices."

Fearing perhaps Eleanor had suffered a concussion and the doctor had misread the tests, with great concern Bob gently placed a kiss on her forehead. "Why don't I take you back to the hospital? Perhaps they should have kept you overnight for observation."

Eleanor pulled free of his grasp. "You're patronizing me. Why can't you believe me?"

A frown creased his forehead. "You tell me of three women named Faith, Hope, and Charity who took you to visit your life while you were in the hospital, and you ask me why I don't believe you? El, you were unconscious for only a short time. Are you sure you didn't imagine this whole thing?"

Placing her hands on her hips, she glared at him. "I'm really not sure how they came to me, but this I do know: Because of their visits and what they showed to me, I'm a changed person, Bob—changed for the better. I'm going to do things differently from now on. I'm going to be a better person, one who people will respect, and I'm going to share my wealth with those who are in need."

Still doubting she was her true self, Bob gave her a skeptical look. "You're talking about a pretty drastic change."

Taking her hands from her hips, she nodded. "I know. And you probably don't think I mean it, but I do."

"I want to believe you. I've always thought, under that independent, self-made woman was that shy little girl I once knew." He leaned against a counter and crossed his arms over his chest. "I know you think it's silly, but I've always felt responsible for you, El. Ever since that day at the pond. I can't help it." Unable to hold it back, Bob gave her a shy grin. "I don't know what I would have done if you'd fallen through the ice and drowned. You—you were my first love. A man never gets over his first love."

Eleanor's expression softened and suddenly she looked like the eight-year-old child he remembered so well, the one he'd risked his life to save.

"You were my first love, too, Bob. But there's one big difference between the two of us. I'm not very proud to admit it, but I never loved Everett. Not like a woman should love the man she marries. I was so selfish and self-centered. I married him because of what he could do for me—and the honor and prestige that went with being the wife of a wealthy businessman. You married Lydia because you loved her. I've never experienced that kind of love with another person."

"I did love her, El. I loved her deeply. I can't tell you how much I've missed her. She was a wonderful wife and a terrific mother."

"Do you—do you think you could ever love another woman?"

Surprised by her strange question, Bob stared at her. "I know Lydia wanted me to marry again someday. Why do you ask?"

"Because. . ." With trembling lips and her eyes filling with tears, Eleanor reached out and took his hand. "Because I've never stopped loving you."

He watched as her hand flew to cover her mouth, as if she'd never meant to let those words slip out. "I—I love you, too, El. You're my best friend."

Her brows rose. "That's it? Only as a friend?"

He let out a long, slow sigh before answering. "Okay. More than as a friend."

"How—how much more?"

The crushed look on her face tore at his heart. He backed away a step and stared at her. "You're putting me on the spot, you know. I'm not sure the two of us should be talking about such things."

Eleanor rushed to him and threw her arms around him. "Please, Bob, I have to know. Could you ever love another woman? Could you ever love me?"

"Come on, El, don't ask me a question like that. You and I—we could never spend our lives together. You wouldn't be happy with me. We—we come from different worlds, but that's not the main reason." Warily, he placed a placating hand on her shoulder. "I don't mean to offend you, but—well—even if we could work out our differences, you've drifted a long way from God, and God is the center of my life. I could never—"

Cupping her hand over his, she smiled up at him through misty lashes. "But you don't understand! Charity convinced me I was a sinner! I've already asked God to forgive me, and He did! I've turned my life over to Him. I didn't understand what that meant when I was a child. But I do now, and I want to live for God like you do!"

Tilting his head, Bob narrowed his eyes. "You're not just saying this to impress me? You've really gotten your life straightened out with God? Because taking a step like that is the biggest decision you'll ever make. You shouldn't joke about it."

As if Eleanor couldn't contain her smile and the joy she felt in her heart at just voicing her new faith in God, she grinned up at him. "God is here," she said, planting her hand over her heart. "Right here, dwelling within me, helping me do His will. That's the reason I wanted to do something for your wonderful family this Christmas. God has blessed me with so much, even though I haven't deserved any of it. He has put the desire in my heart to share my blessings."

"You're serious, aren't you?"

Looking both elated and sad, she nodded. "Yes. Even if you feel you can't love me, you must believe me, because I am telling you the truth about this. Though I wandered far away and, at times, even doubted His existence, I have come back to the God I accepted as a child and made my peace with Him."

Her words were exactly what he'd prayed for and longed to hear. Snatching her up in his arms and spinning her around, Bob smiled into her face. "My precious, precious El. You have no idea how happy this makes me. I've been praying for you for so long, I'd begun to wonder if God was hearing my prayers."

"You've been a shining example to me of what a real Christian's life should be."

"God has been good to me, El. I love Him with all my heart."

"And it's obvious to all who know you." Eleanor cupped her hands on his cheeks and gazed up at him. "You never answered me, Bob, and I need to know. I've told you the truth, and I expect the truth from you." Gulping, she asked again, "Could you ever love another woman? Could you ever love me?"

twelve

Thrilled his prayers had been heard after all and Eleanor had made her peace with God, Bob searched his heart for an answer to her question. If he told Eleanor the truth that, though he'd married Lydia, he'd never stopped loving her, that truth could be the catalyst to separate them even further. He was nothing but a lowly accountant—one of her employees. They could never have a life together. He'd always be subordinate to her. A situation like that would never work—for either of them. Under those conditions, how could they even continue to work together? Expressing his love for her could leave him without a job.

"Please, Bob, I have to know."

Though it may cost him everything, he had to answer with the truth and trust God would take care of him and his family. Clasping his hands over hers, he drew them to his lips and tenderly kissed her fingertips. "Of course, I could love you, El. I've never stopped loving you, but don't you see? Love is not enough. Even though you and I are both Christians, there are so many things that still separate us. You've never wanted a family—"

"But I do now!"

"Perhaps, with this newfound love for God, you only think you do, but do you have any idea what is involved in being a parent? You can't buy the love of a child, El, even with the wonderful clothing and toys you've selected for them. Yes, children want those things, but they soon tire of them and they end up in the closet or the toy box, nearly forgotten.

What children want—what I want—is a full-time wife and mother. One who puts God first, her husband second, and her children third."

The look on her face ripped at his heart but these things had to be said. "You're a successful businesswoman, El. You could never turn your back on all of that, no more than I could give up my family to become your husband."

"I—I love you, Bob. More than words can express. I can't lose you twice!"

He wrapped his arms around her and drew her close. "I love you, too, El. But—if we were honest—we'd admit there is no future for us as a couple."

Eleanor wiped at the tears flowing down her cheeks and, turning her head away, added three more toys to the cart then motioned toward the front of the store. "I'm finished here. Let's go."

Silently, they moved through the semidarkened store and out the front door, with Eleanor locking it securely behind her. Bob loaded the gifts she'd selected into his car, tied the bicycle on top, and then crawled into the seat beside her. "I'm sorry, El. The last thing I wanted to do was hurt you, but I'm hurt, too. You have no idea how much I'd like to spend the rest of my life with you, as your husband, but I see no way it can happen."

She wrapped her coat tightly about her and smiled up at him. "Don't count on that, Bob Rachette. I remember your mother teaching me a verse about how God moves in mysterious ways, His wonders to perform. I think we should just give it all over to Him."

Bob turned to her in surprise. "Wow, I never expected to hear words like those coming from you."

❧

Eleanor felt herself beaming. She was now truly a child of God, and although she wanted so much to be Mrs. Robert

Rachette, the thing she wanted most of all was to be in the center of God's will.

By the time they reached his house it was past eleven o'clock. After unloading the car, they placed Eleanor's presents under the simply decorated tree alongside the few meager ones Bob had already placed there. Not having had time or enough paper and ribbons to wrap them, he covered them with a sheet, then showed Eleanor to her room. Shyly, he kissed her on the forehead and said good night.

She donned the plain flannel nightgown someone had laid on the bed, which had probably belonged to Lydia, then sat gazing about the tiny room Bob Jr. had vacated for the night, visualizing what it would be like to hear that young boy call her "Mother." Shaking her head to clear the thought, she switched off the lamp and climbed beneath the quilt. Soon she heard Bob come down the hall and go into his room. It was all she could do the keep from getting up and knocking on his door to plead with him to reconsider his decision. But knowing Bob Jr. was sleeping in there with his father, she remained in her bed and soon fell asleep.

❧

"Wake up, Mrs. Scrooge!"

Eleanor's eyes snapped open, and she found herself nose to nose with smiling, five-year-old Megan.

Megan tugged on her hand. "Daddy said you gotta get up now. It's almost time to open our presents!"

She noticed a pale blue chenille robe draped over a chair. Eleanor quickly climbed out of bed and put it on, ignoring the designer suit she'd hung in the closet before retiring.

Megan held out her hand. "Daddy always puts a new toothbrush in our Christmas stocking. You can have mine."

With a terrible taste in her mouth from not brushing her teeth before going to bed, Eleanor eagerly took the gift from the child. "Thank you, Megan. That's very nice of you.

I promise I'll get you a new toothbrush as soon as I can."

Megan sat down on the edge of the bed. "That's okay. It can be your Christmas present. I'll wait for you."

After giving the little girl an honest smile, Eleanor checked to make sure Bob was nowhere around then moved toward the tiny bathroom at the end of the hall. One look in the mirror made her shudder. Her beautiful upswept hairdo was a mess and, other than a few remaining telltale bits of mascara, her makeup had disappeared. After brushing her teeth and washing her face with the bar of soap on the sink, she pulled the pins from her hair, let it fall softly to her shoulders, and gave it a good brushing with a brush she found on a nearby shelf.

"This is Eleanor Scrooge?" she asked herself, smiling into the mirror. "The woman who always looked her best, who went to the beauty shop twice a week?" Glancing down at the simple gown and robe, she let out a giggle. "Um, not bad. Is this the way I'd look if I were Mrs. Robert Rachette?"

The door opened a crack and a tiny face appeared. "Are you ready?"

With one last glance in the mirror, Eleanor accepted the child's hand, and the two moved into the living room where the rest of the family was already assembled.

"I don't understand, Daddy," young Ginny was saying. "Why is there a sheet on the floor under the tree?"

Bob sent a grin Eleanor's way as she sat down on the sofa beside him. "You'll find out soon enough, but right now it's time to read the Christmas story."

Eleanor watched as he opened the big Bible on his lap and began to read in his magnificent deep voice, the slightly graying hair at his temples giving him a distinguished look. She recognized the story immediately, though it had been years since she'd heard Mr. Rachette read it. It was Luke's account of Jesus' birth. Looking from one child to the other, she was amazed at how they each paid such rapt attention.

"I love Jesus," Megan said, smiling up at her father as she sat on his lap. "If Joseph had brought Mary to our house, we'd have given them a bed and something to eat, wouldn't we, Daddy?"

Bob nodded. "Yes, Megan, we sure would have, but it was in God's plan that His Son be born in a manger. You see, it had been foretold that the Messiah would be born, but no one expected He would be born in a stable."

Megan wiggled off her father's lap and, much to Eleanor's surprise, climbed into her lap, snuggling down into her arms. Eleanor felt like a queen. Never had she experienced the feelings that were flooding through her at that moment as she gazed at Bob's little family.

Bob stopped his reading. "Megan, you shouldn't bother Mrs. Scrooge."

Eleanor wrapped her arms tightly about the little girl. "Let her stay. I love holding her."

He gave her a quizzical smile, then continued with the story. Finally, after reaching the part in Matthew about the wise men, he closed the Bible and bowed his head, as did each of the children, as naturally as if Bible reading and praying were a regular part of their lives.

"Father God," he said with such sincerity it gave Eleanor goose bumps, "we come to You this Christmas morning with grateful hearts. Not for the gifts we are about to receive, but for the gift You have given us. The gift of Your own dear Son, who lived an exemplary life, was rejected by men, died a cruel death on the cross, and rose again that we might spend eternity in heaven with You. We praise You for all the blessings You constantly pour out upon us. You know the needs and desires of our hearts. Have Your will in our lives. Mold us and make us what You want us to be."

He reached across and took Eleanor's hand in his, giving it a squeeze. "And thank You for letting us share our Christmas with Eleanor. May none of us ever forget the true meaning of Christmas. In Your precious name we ask all these things. Amen."

She wished this moment could go on forever. There was something about being in this home, on this day, which was almost magical. "May I say something?"

Bob nodded. "Of course you may. You're a guest in our home, and we're happy to have you here to share the celebration of Christ's birthday with us."

Eleanor stroked little Megan's hair nervously. She'd been a guest speaker numerous times at both public and business occasions and had never been nervous about what she had to say. But here in Bob's house, with him and his children, she found it difficult to put her thoughts into the words that would convey her true feelings. "When I was a little younger than Bob Jr., I accepted Christ as my Savior. But as I grew older, I forgot about Him and turned away from Him. All these years, I've ignored His very existence, never praying or even believing in Him. But yesterday, something wonderful happened. Three ladies—"

She sent a glance toward Bob, knowing he doubted the vision, dream, or whatever she had experienced. "Three ladies helped me see my life for what it was. Empty, lonely, and filled with things that didn't matter and had no lasting value. Because of them, I took a long, hard look at that life, and you know what? I decided to make some drastic changes. I want to live for God now, however He wants me to live."

"El—"

"Let me finish, Bob, please." She gave each child a caring smile. "I thought I was rich, but I found out I was really the one who was poor. I had things—things that were nice, but I had no one to share them with. You children are far richer than I. Your father loves you and would do anything to protect you." Eleanor did her best but could not suppress a tear, her emotions taking over against her will. "I know you lost your mother, and I'm so sorry, but her love still surrounds you. You children, though you may not realize it now, bear the love she has given you. I hope you'll always love God and keep Him first in your life."

Ginny, who was seated alone on the floor at the end of the sofa and had remained silent, reached out and took Eleanor's hand in hers. "I'm so happy for you, Mrs. Scrooge. He's a wonderful God. I don't know what I would do without Him."

Eleanor couldn't help staring at the girl, her natural beauty marred by the terrible red birthmark on her lower cheek. There was something about Ginny that reminded her of herself at that age. . . . A sadness. An almost melancholy look. Why hadn't she done something to help the girl? She'd known about that birthmark for years, yet she'd never been interested enough to even ask about it. Holding Ginny's hand tightly in hers, Eleanor smiled through her tears. "You know what, Ginny? God has spoken to my heart. I'm going to make sure you get the treatments you deserve."

Letting out a gasp, Bob reached across and grabbed hold of her wrist. "Don't, El. Don't get her hopes up. She's been disappointed so many times."

"She's not going to be disappointed this time," she assured him, for the first time feeling a great need to do something positive for someone else. "God gave me all this money. Perhaps this is one way He would have me spend it."

"You have no idea of the expense involved, El. Maybe you'd better reconsider."

Eleanor lifted her chin resolutely. "There is no need for me to reconsider. If it takes everything I have, Ginny is going to have her dream fulfilled. It's my Christmas present to her. You give me whatever information you have as to what doctor and hospital can perform the treatments, and I'll call the first thing tomorrow morning and get the ball rolling."

"But, El—"

Eleanor motioned toward the tree. "Isn't it about time your family opened their presents?"

෴

After a glance toward Ginny, Bob nodded, feeling a touch of sadness as he pulled the sheet from the many presents that lay on the floor beneath the decorated tree. This was going to be the best Christmas his family had ever had, but what they were about to receive hadn't come from him, nor would he be able next year, or any year, to provide such lavish gifts. "Eleanor," he said, turning to her with a forced smile, "perhaps, since the presents you have brought are not wrapped and tagged, you will want to be the one to give them to the children."

Eleanor shook her head. "No, Bob, I want you to do it. You and I selected those presents together. They're from both of us."

Her answer caught him off guard. The old Eleanor would never have shared the spotlight with anyone. She would have demanded full credit for what she had done. Perhaps she was telling him the truth after all. Perhaps she really had decided to make major changes in her life and had gotten her relationship straightened out with God.

The love he felt for her rose in his heart. Though he tried to tamp it down, he couldn't. He longed to take her into his arms and hold her close. *God, can this really be happening? You know how much it hurt the first time I lost Eleanor. Surely You don't expect me to lose her a second time. Please show me Your will. Is there a way? Could Eleanor and I be happy as husband and wife? Could she be the kind of mother my children deserve? I'm so confused. Only You can work this out. Please, God, I need direction. Don't let me make a mistake that could hurt all of us.*

He felt Eleanor's hand on his arm, and when he turned to face her, she smiled at him with the most angelic smile he'd ever seen on an earthly woman.

"Go on," she said, giving his shoulder a slight nudge. "Your family is waiting."

By nine o'clock that night, with Eleanor's help, the mess in the kitchen from the turkey dinner Kari and Ginny had prepared had been cleaned up, the presents put away, and the house put back to normal.

"Merry Christmas, Mrs. Scrooge," Bob told her as they sat on the sofa watching the lights blinking on the Christmas tree.

Sitting on the sofa next to Bob, Eleanor stared at the tree. "It's beautiful. All the Christmas trees I've had since I married Everett were ones designed by a design team and assembled in my home, but none of them could compare with this tree. I love the ornaments the children made, and I love being in your home," she told him, leaning her head against his shoulder with a contented sigh and snuggling in close to him. "Merry Christmas, Mr. Rachette."

"My family has loved having you here. You've made Christmas very special. Oh, not with the extravagant gifts you brought, but just by being here. Thank you for making this day one we'll never forget." Still not sure if he dare let their relationship go any farther, he leaned his head against hers, drinking in the sweet fragrance of her perfume. "I promise I'll get right on your Valentine promotion first thing in the morning."

&

"I know you will. You always keep your word. I guess I should be going," Eleanor said, hating to leave the closeness she and Bob were sharing and the sanctity of the Rachette home. What a day she'd had. Though the children had loved the magnificent gifts she had brought for them, much to her amazement, they had been equally pleased with the few things their father had purchased for them. "You have such a wonderful family, Bob," she told him sincerely. "I—I hate to leave them."

"You could stay another night."

Though she longed to stay, she shook her head. "No, the

doctor said I only needed someone to be with me twenty-four hours. It's time I went home. I don't want to wear out my welcome."

"You're sure you can't stay?"

"I'd love to stay forever, but I'd better go. I'm sure Bob Jr. would like his bed back."

Bob rose then extended his hand and pulled her to her feet. "You will come back again soon. You have a standing invitation, you know." He assisted her into her coat then pulled on his own coat and led her to the door, wrapping his arm around her as they walked. "Better button up; it's cold out there."

She leaned into him as they walked to the car, relishing their closeness and wondering if this would the last time he'd hold her like this. "I've had a wonderful time."

"Me, too." He opened the car door, waited until she was seated, then rushed around to the other side. "You don't have to do it, you know."

She gave him a sideways glance as he backed the car out of the driveway. "Do what?"

"Take care of Ginny's treatments."

"But I want to!"

"God doesn't expect works, El."

"I know that! Surely, you don't think I believe I can work my way to heaven!"

He reached across and capped her hand with his. "I didn't mean to offend you. That was a stupid statement. I just didn't want you to—"

"Get your daughter's hopes up and then desert her? Like I did you?"

Turning away and training his eyes on the road, he nodded. "Yeah, I guess so. Disappointment hurts, El. I know."

"Stop the car!"

He brought it to a screeching halt. "Why? What's the matter?"

Her eyes narrowed, and her face pinched with determination. "You and I need to get something straight, Bob Rachette. I love you—more deeply and honestly than you can imagine. Even though I've only known your children for barely twenty-four hours, I love them. But, most of all, I love God."

"But you—"

"Be quiet and listen, please! I've changed. The old Eleanor Scrooge is dead. Dead! Do you hear me? The new Eleanor is nothing like her. The new Eleanor loves God with all her heart and wants to do His will." She latched onto his arm and held it tightly in her grasp. "I want you, Bob Rachette! I want to be your wife! I want to be a mother to your children! I know I could never replace Lydia. I wouldn't even try, but I would be the best mother I could be."

"El, I—"

"Pride! That's all that's keeping us apart. Your silly, stupid, ridiculous pride. You can't imagine being married to the woman who owns and manages the company you work for, am I right?"

"Yes, I guess so, but—"

"I've been thinking about this all day. I did a terrible thing when Everett died. As you know, Everett had three nephews—his sister's children. Before he married me, he had it in his will that, upon his death, he was leaving each of them one third of his fortune. I'm ashamed to admit it, but the first thing I did after we got back from our honeymoon was to make sure he changed that will, leaving everything to me. Because of me and my selfishness, those nephews didn't get a penny."

"I—I didn't know."

Even in the dim light of the car, Eleanor could see Bob's eyes narrow. She could only imagine what he thought of her. "Other than the nephews and Everett's lawyers, very few people did. The nephews tried to break the will, but I'd made sure it was unbreakable."

"Why are you telling me this now?"

"Because I've made a decision. After I find out what Ginny's treatments, the travel, hotel, hospital, and other expenses are going to be and I've set that money aside, I'm going to make things right and try to undo the wrongs I've done. I'm going to keep Scrooge's, but along with a sincere apology I'm going to give his nephews the rest of the estate I inherited from Everett, including the mansion. I've met them, Bob. Even though I'd said terrible things about them, they're nice boys from a good family, and I know they'll be good stewards and not squander his wealth."

Bob stared at her. "But why? Why would you do such a thing?"

Eleanor scooted closer to him and gazed up into his eyes. "Because I want to be Mrs. Robert Rachette, that's why! I'm only keeping Scrooge's department store because you've helped me build it and are an important part of it."

He grabbed onto her arm so tightly she let out a little squeal. "El, you can't be serious! You'd give up all that wealth to become my wife?"

"I'd give up everything to become your wife."

"Oh, El, I've tried to fight it, but I love you so much it—"

She quickly placed a finger across his lips. "Shh! Before you say another word, I have to tell you something else. If you'll have me, I'm stepping down and becoming only an advisor to Scrooge's, naming someone else to fill my place as CEO. That way I can spend most of my time with the children."

"If I'll have you? You know I want you, El, but—"

"I'm naming you the new CEO of Scrooge's."

His jaw dropping, Bob reared back and stared at her. "Me? I'm not qualified. I could never be Scrooge's CEO."

Eleanor poked a finger at his chest. "You, my darling, are the perfect one to take my place. You know everything there is to know about Scrooge's finances, the business, and the new Web site. You get along with everyone, and everyone loves you. And, although you'll be in complete charge, I'll be available if you need me. Think about it, Bob. Think what our marriage would mean to us—to your children."

"But, El, do you really think you could do that? Turn Scrooge's over to someone else?"

"Trust me. Nothing would make me happier than to turn it all over to you. I'm tired of my life, Bob. Tired of going to work each day and coming home to an empty house."

"But that store has been your baby—your life. Maybe I'd do something wrong, and the sales would—"

"Bob! Forget all those negative things! I want to be your wife! I want to be a mother to Kari, Ginny, Bob Jr., Megan, and little Janelle. Just tell me! Do you love me? Do you want me to marry you? Come on here—give me some help! I want this more than anything in the world, but please don't make me beg!"

To her surprise, Bob bowed his head and remained silent.

Finally, Eleanor could stand it no longer. Almost to the point of irritation, she called out, "What are you doing? Say something. Anything!"

With a toothy grin, he lifted his face. "I was praying."

"Don't keep me in suspense! Did God give you any answers?"

"Yes, He did." Bob reached out and pulled her to him.

"Quit teasing me! What did He say?"

After brushing his lips across hers, he kissed her tenderly, then murmured, "He said I should ask you to become my wife."

epilogue

One month later

"Venual malformations, or port-wine stains as we call them, are always present at birth and can range from pale pink to dark purple in color," Dr. Kinard, the director of the Vascular Anomalies Team at the hospital in Little Rock explained as he examined Ginny's cheek. "Your daughter is fortunate. Hers is one of the lighter ones."

"And you can treat it, right?" Eleanor asked, holding tightly to Ginny's hand. "It can be removed?"

Dr. Kinard leaned in for a better look. "It's important that you know, although laser therapy is successfully used to remove a port-wine stain, the treatment will only be a temporary fix. Since the deficiency is in the nervous system, in time the blood will repool in the affected area, and the birthmark will reappear."

Bob nodded. "We understand that, Doctor, and we're prepared to deal with it. So is Ginny. Aren't you, sweetheart?"

Ginny smiled up at the doctor. "Yes. I know it's going to be painful, but I really want to get rid of my birthmark."

Eleanor bent and kissed the top of Ginny's head. "We're prepared to do whatever is necessary. Ginny is such a sweet child. She deserves to have a normal life."

"Just wanted us to all understand what we're dealing with here," the doctor went on. "I have no magic potions. Once a port-wine stain is lasered, it is extremely important at the first sign of recurrence that she has additional treatments

168

to keep it faded. She may have to have maintenance laser treatments the rest of her life. She may not. Only God knows. Fortunately, we're getting to her early enough to, hopefully, prevent cobbling of the skin and thickening and darkening of the stain. Low-grade ones, like Ginny's, progress at a slower rate than high-grade."

Encouraged by the doctor's words, Eleanor asked, "How soon can you start?"

"How about two weeks from Monday? That's the earliest I can work her in."

"Can Eleanor stay with me while I have my treatments?" Ginny asked, clinging to Eleanor's arm. "I—I want her with me."

The girl's words touched Eleanor so deeply she began to cry. One glance toward Bob told her they had touched him deeply, too.

Dr. Kinard bobbed his head. "Of course you can. Most girls want their mothers to be with them at a time like that."

Smiling, Bob grabbed Eleanor's arm and gave it a squeeze. "We'll both be here."

After the nurse set the appointment and gave them a few pamphlets to read, arm in arm, the three walked out of the doctor's office and toward the car they'd rented at the airport.

Bob wrapped his arm around Eleanor as Ginny, filled with excitement, surged on ahead of them across the parking lot. "Well, thanks to you, it's finally going to happen. Ginny's birthmark will soon be history."

El frowned at him. "Don't say that, Bob. I have no reason to be thanked. We're going to be a family, which means we're doing this thing together."

"My kids love you, you know. How did you win them over so quickly?"

She gave him a playful shrug. "I guess they could see how much I loved them."

He pulled her even closer and whispered in her ear. "You sure you don't want to wait until after Ginny's treatments to tie the knot with me?"

Feeling as though she would burst with love for this man, she lifted her face to his and gazed into his eyes. "And take a chance on letting you get away? Absolutely not!"

He gave her an impish smile. "Then the wedding is still on for this Sunday?"

"Only if you'll give me one thing."

Bob hugged her tight. "Me give you one thing? You already have everything a woman could wish for. What could I possibly give you that you don't already have?"

Eleanor tingled at his touch. It felt so good to have his arms wrapped around her. "It's something I want very much, my dear husband-to-be, and you are the only one who can give it to me."

Bob responded with a puzzled expression and a raised brow. "Only *I* can give it to you?"

"Yes, sweetheart, only you. No one else. And what I'm about to ask of you would make me the happiest woman in the world."

Still holding her tight, his puzzled expression turned into a frown. "I have no idea what you're talking about, El, but if it is within my power to give it to you—"

Eleanor rose on tiptoe and planted an adoring kiss on the cheek of the only man she'd ever loved. The man she'd loved since she was a little girl. Gazing dreamily into his eyes, she answered in her sweetest voice, "Nothing, except becoming your wife, would make me any happier than adding a sixth child to the Rachette household! I want us to have a baby!"

A Letter To Our Readers

Dear Reader:

In order that we might better contribute to your reading enjoyment, we would appreciate your taking a few minutes to respond to the following questions. We welcome your comments and read each form and letter we receive. When completed, please return to the following:

Fiction Editor
Heartsong Presents
PO Box 719
Uhrichsville, Ohio 44683

1. Did you enjoy reading *Bah Humbug, Mrs. Scrooge* by Joyce Livingston?
   ❏ Very much! I would like to see more books by this author!
   ❏ Moderately. I would have enjoyed it more if

   _____

   _____

   _____

2. Are you a member of **Heartsong Presents**? ❏ Yes ❏ No
   If no, where did you purchase this book? _____

   _____

3. How would you rate, on a scale from 1 (poor) to 5 (superior), the cover design? _____

4. On a scale from 1 (poor) to 10 (superior), please rate the following elements.

   ____ Heroine   ____ Plot
   ____ Hero   ____ Inspirational theme
   ____ Setting   ____ Secondary characters

5. These characters were special because? _____
_____
_____

6. How has this book inspired your life? _____
_____
_____

7. What settings would you like to see covered in future
   Heartsong Presents books? _____
_____
_____

8. What are some inspirational themes you would like to see
   treated in future books? _____
_____
_____

9. Would you be interested in reading other **Heartsong
   Presents** titles? ❑ Yes   ❑ No

10. Please check your age range:
    ❑ Under 18   ❑ 18-24
    ❑ 25-34   ❑ 35-45
    ❑ 46-55   ❑ Over 55

Name _____
Occupation _____
Address _____
City, State, Zip _____

Heartong

HEARTSONG PRESENTS TITLES AVAILABLE NOW:

(If ordering from this page, please remember to include it with the order form.)

Presents

Great Inspirational Romance at a Great Price!

Heartsong Presents books are inspirational romances in
contemporary and historical settings, designed to give you an
enjoyable, spirit-lifting reading experience. You can choose
wonderfully written titles from some of today's best authors like
Hannah Alexander, Andrea Boeshaar, Yvonne Lehman, Tracie
Peterson, and many others.

When ordering quantities less than twelve, above titles are $2.97 each.
Not all titles may be available at time of order.

HEARTSONG
P R E S E N T S

If you love Christian romance…

$10.⁹⁹

You'll love Heartsong Presents' inspiring and faith-filled romances by today's very best Christian authors…DiAnn Mills, Wanda E. Brunstetter, and Yvonne Lehman, to mention a few!

When you join Heartsong Presents, you'll enjoy 4 brand-new mass market, 176-page books—two contemporary and two historical—that will build you up in your faith when you discover God's role in every relationship you read about!

Imagine…four new romances every four weeks—with men and women like you who long to meet the one God has chosen as the love of their lives…all for the low price of $10.99 postpaid.

To join, simply visit www.heartsong presents.com or complete the coupon below and mail it to the address provided.

Mass Market 176 Pages

✂ -

YES! Sign me up for Heartsong!

NEW MEMBERSHIPS WILL BE SHIPPED IMMEDIATELY!
Send no money now. We'll bill you only $10.99 postpaid with your first shipment of four books. Or for faster action, call 1-740-922-7280.

NAME _____

ADDRESS _____

CITY _____ STATE _____ ZIP _____

MAIL TO: HEARTSONG PRESENTS, P.O. Box 721, Uhrichsville, Ohio 44683
or sign up at **WWW.HEARTSONGPRESENTS.COM**